THE ELEPHANT &
THE TORTOISE
&
OTHER STORIES

Publications from
The Scheherazade Foundation

THE ELEPHANT &
THE TORTOISE
&
OTHER STORIES

Edited & Introduced by

TAHIR SHAH

The Scheherazade Foundation

The Scheherazade Foundation CIC
85 Great Portland Street
London
W1W 7LT
United Kingdom
www.SF.Charity
info@SF.Charity

First published by The Scheherazade Foundation CIC, 2023

THE ELEPHANT & THE TORTOISE
&
OTHER STORIES

The Elephant & the Tortoise
Bulu Tales from Kamerun
Journal of American Folklore
1912

The Story of the Fisherman
One Thousand & One Nights
Andrew Lang
Longmans, Green & Co.
1918

How Footbinding Started
A Chinese Wonder Book
Norman Hinsdale Pitman
E. P. Dutton & Co.
1919

Dinewan the Emu, & Goomblegubbon
the Bustard
Australian Legendary Tales
David Nutt Ltd.
1896

The Lassie & Her Godmother
East of the Sun & West of the Moon
Peter Christen Asbjørnsen & Jørgen
Engebretsen Moe
George H. Doran Co.
1922

Silver Bells
Tales from the Lands of Nuts & Grapes
Charles Sellers
The Leadenhall Press
1888

The She-bear
Stories From Pentamerone
Giambattista Basile
David Bogue
1634

How the Monkey Became a Trickster
Fairy Tales from Brazil
Elsie Spicer Eells
Dodd, Mead and Co.
1917

The Fall of the Spider Man
Canadian Fairy Tales
Cyrus Macmillan
S. B. Gundy
1922

Why the Bat is Ashamed to be Seen in
the Daytime
Folk Stories from Southern Nigeria
Elphinstone Dayrell
Longmans, Green & Co.
1910

Aponibolinayen & the Sun
Philippine Folk Tales
Mabel Cook Cole
A.C. McClurg & Co.
1916

The Tale of the Silver Saucer & the
Transparent Apple
Old Peter's Russian Tales
Arthur Ransome
Thomas Nelson & Sons Ltd.
1916

The Fairies of Caragonan
Welsh Fairy-Tales & Other Stories
P. H. Emerson
D. Nutt & Ltd.
1894

Clever Manka: The Story of a Girl Who
Knew What to Say
*The Shoemaker's Apron: A Second Book
of Czechoslovak Fairy Tales & Folk Tales*
Parker Fillmore
Harcourt, Brace and Co.
1920

The Little White Cat
Irish Fairy Tales
Edmond Leamy
M. A. Gill & Son. Ltd.
1906

The various authors listed above assert the right to be identified as the Authors of
the Work in accordance with the Copyright, Designs and Patents Act 1988.
A CIP catalogue record for this title is available from the British Library.

ISBN 978-1-915311-04-7

CONTENTS

Series Introduction

FROM EARLIEST CHILDHOOD, I was told stories.

Of course, I was – most children are told stories.

After all, telling children stories is one of the foundations that makes their early experiences a childhood.

But as I think back to the first years of my own life, I find myself reeling from the sheer quantity of stories my infant ears took in.

Whereas other children my age were told stories for amusement, my parents (and the people they associated with) recounted the endless streams of tales for a different reason.

In their opinion, stories – and the ability to tell them – were part of an ancient alchemy... a way of processing complex ideas, of solving problems, and of developing the human mind.

My father, the writer and thinker Idries Shah, believed that folklore was the single most important breakthrough ever developed by the human species. The way he saw it, the rise of stories was as consequential as the development of the languages in which they were told.

He would say that, without stories and storytelling, humanity would never have evolved in the way that it has – and that the folktales, which form a bedrock of ancient societies, are more precious than any physical artefact unearthed on an archaeological dig.

As the years of my own childhood slipped by, I found myself unbothered to work out the hidden layers within treasuries of stories – what my father called 'instruction manuals to the world.' Like everyone else, I simply absorbed the individual tales, delighting in them.

And that's it – the key point, the genius of stories and storytelling.

It's a thing I only grasped in adulthood… something that fascinates me deeply.

In the same way you can jump into a car and drive across the country without giving a second thought to the engine or how it works, you can appreciate stories without understanding the hidden layers and devices that make them what they are.

Stories are all around us.

They're in the TV and movies we so adore, in the video games we play, and of course in the books we read. They're in newspapers and magazines, too; in the conversations we share with old friends, and with new ones. They're on our mobile phones, in aeroplanes, in submarines, and even in our dreams.

Our obsession with, and craving for, stories rests squarely with the way we are so absorbed by them, just as it does with the way we don't need to continually consider how and why they work.

Throughout my life, I've devoted an increasing amount of time to gathering stories from all corners of the world.

It began in my late teens, when I began to criss-cross the continents in a crazed preoccupation with folklore. I developed a first-hand love affair with societies that, over millennia, gave birth to their own astonishing traditions of stories and storytelling.

Most of the time, when reading or listening to stories, we forget that these tales have been shaped through the passage of time. Like pebbles in a river smoothed by rushing waters, they were honed through centuries of telling and retelling.

When I was twelve years old, my father published a masterwork, *World Tales*. The first edition was very large and featured hundreds of original illustrations. The book was unlike any that had come before, for it detailed the provenance and history of each story told.

At bedtime one night, he presented me with an advanced copy. For as long as I could remember, my father had been talking about the project.

Having an actual copy in my hands at last was thrilling beyond words.

Peering down at me sternly, my father said:

'This is far more than a book, Tahir Jan. It's the foundation stone of a great building... a building that *is* human culture. As you grow older, and as you go out into the world, you will understand that the folklores contained between the covers of *World Tales* have brought amusement and educated, and have solved problems when they were needed most of all.'

My father was right.

When I eventually headed out into the wilds of the world for the first time, I discovered the stories contained in *World Tales* for myself, along with a great many more. Just as he said, the stories published in his treasury were the warp and weft threads of society. Stories are the matrix on which culture itself is based – a framework that enables daily life to continue as smoothly as it does.

In this series of books, we have drawn together stories from all over the world. It's a mission begun decades ago by *World Tales*.

Some of the pieces will be known to you, and others will not.

Some will be easy to comprehend, while others will be challenging, or even nonsensical.

I'd now like to note something else…

The Occidental world seems to assume stories must appear in certain regimented ways – presented with a well-defined beginning, a middle, and an end. You know what I mean: the protagonist winning against all odds, and the happy ending to it all.

In the ancient tradition of teaching stories, the kind recounted for an eternity around campfires in the desert and in longhouses deep in the jungle, there's no such standardisation.

Rather, there's usually a hotchpotch of conflicting threads: stories without a straight linear narrative but with an underlying turbulence that gets the reader, or the listener, to sit up and think.

At The Scheherazade Foundation, we are preoccupied with the way we can extract knowledge from stories – either deliberately, or in a less structured way.

We hold the firm opinion that, in order to remove the marrow from the bone stories are best served up in the way as they were passed from one generation to the next throughout human history.

In this series, we have drawn together tales that were gathered in particular during the nineteenth and early twentieth centuries. Spanning a vast range of cultures, they offer an extraordinary glimpse into the societies from which they are drawn – societies that were often changed shortly afterwards by social upheaval, technologies, and war.

Indeed, the fact any of them were recorded at all is a thing of wonder.

Intriguingly, some of the tales will now appear dated because vocabulary and writing styles have altered. But the fact that they seem old-fashioned is of great interest – proof of the way stories are constantly changing and evolving from one era to the next.

Over the last thirty years, I've gathered hundreds of tales on my own journeys, most of them spoken directly into my ears by storytellers and fellow travellers, by wizened old men in the middle of nowhere, and by anyone else good enough to indulge my pleas.

On all those zigzagging adventures, one story sticks out, tantalising me whenever I turn it around my head.

It was called 'The Man Who Turned into a Cat.'

The reason I mention it here is not because it was an especially fine tale, but rather because, from that moment, it affected the way I perceive the world.

It was as though I were a lock and that, by hearing the tale, a key had been slipped into me and turned.

Since first receiving it, I've never been quite the same, my state of consciousness having been flipped inside out.

The fellow traveller who recounted 'The Man Who Turned into a Cat' was lost in shadow, no more than a fragment of his left cheek protruding shyly into the light.

We were sitting on low divans in a teahouse in the ancient Afghan city of Herat.

When the tale had been whispered, I sat there in silence for a long while.

'What have you done to me?' I asked after a long pause.

The fellow traveller offered half a smile.

'*I* didn't do anything,' he replied. 'It's the story that's affected you – a story that I myself first heard when I was a child playing in the orchards of Balkh.'

Peering into the shadow, my eyes widened.

'I don't understand,' I said feebly. 'After all, it's not an especially grand story. There wasn't even a jinn.'

The traveller's mouth eased out from the shadows.

Very slowly, it grinned.

'Tales containing the greatest sustenance for a soul speak in the softest voice,' he said.

Tahir Shah

The Elephant & the Tortoise

ONCE UPON A time the Tortoise and the Elephant went on a journey, and they said one to the other, 'Let us go and visit Zambe, the son of Mebe'e!'

Thereupon they started on their journey; and when they came to a river, they stopped and took a bath. When they had finished taking a bath, the Tortoise said to the Elephant, 'Come, my friend, we will take new names for ourselves!'

When the Elephant therefore asked him, 'What names shall we take?'

The Tortoise began, and said, 'My name is "Guests, go to the house"; but the Elephant was named "Guests, remain seated."'

After this the Tortoise said, 'Now we have finished taking new names for ourselves, therefore we will do after this manner: when we have arrived in town, and you hear the people call, "Guests, go to the house," then they are calling me, the Tortoise; but if you hear them call, "Guests, remain seated," then they are calling the Elephant.'

When they had thus finished taking new names, they left the river crossing, and came to the village. Zambe, the son of Mebe'e, was greatly surprised, and said, 'Great guests have come to my village.'

So he killed a fowl and gave it to a woman to cook, and the woman prepared and cooked it.

After this, Zambe called a boy and said to him, 'Go and call my guests from the palaver-house.'

The boy accordingly went to the palaver-house, and called out, 'Guests, go to the house!'

The Tortoise thereupon quickly arose, saying, 'They have called me by my name,' and he said to his children, 'Let us go to the house!'

So the Tortoise and his children went to the house; and they ate the fowl, and saved for the Elephant and his children only a piece of the breast.

Thereupon said Zambe, the son of Mebe'e, 'Perhaps the Elephant despised the fowl.'

So he killed a dog and had it cooked, and said to the boy, 'Go and call my guests from the palaver-house.'

The boy therefore went to the palaver-house and called out.

So the Tortoise again said, 'It is I they are calling,' and he and his children went in and ate the dog, but they kept for the Elephant and his children only a small piece of the dog.

After this Zambe, the son of Mebe'e, killed a sheep and had it prepared also. Then he said again to the boy, 'Go and call my guests from the palaver-house.'

The boy therefore went to the palaver-house and called out, 'Guests, go to the house!'

The Tortoise therefore said again, 'It is my name they have called,' so the Tortoise and his children went to the house, and they ate all of the sheep, keeping for the Elephant and his children only a piece of a leg.

When the next morning had dawned, the Elephant and the Tortoise said one to the other, 'Now we will go home.'

Thereupon Zambe, the son of Mebe'e, took a staff in his hand, and said to the Elephant,

'On the day you arrived here, I killed a fowl but you did not eat of it; after that, I killed a dog, but you did not eat of it, either; so at last I killed a sheep, but never a bite did you eat of it, either; therefore, I want to ask you, what is it you desire that I should now kill for you?'

To this the Elephant replied, and said, 'I did not eat, not because there was too little food, but because we took new names when we came to this town. Therefore, I did in this manner: the name of the Tortoise is "Guests, go to the house"; and the Tortoise always went, because you always called his name, "Guests, go to the house." I did not go because I did not hear you call "Guests, remain seated." If, however, you had called me in that manner, I certainly should have gone.'

Therefore, the people said to the Elephant, 'You are certainly a great big blockhead. Will anyone with any sense ever take such a name for himself?'

Thus did the Tortoise deceive the Elephant.

From: Bulu Tales from Kamerun

The Story of the Fisherman

THERE WAS ONCE upon a time a fisherman so old and so poor, that he could scarcely manage to support his wife and three children.

He went every day to fish very early, and each day he made a rule not to throw his nets more than four times. He started out one morning by moonlight and came to the seashore. He undressed and threw his nets, and as he was drawing them towards the bank, he felt a great weight. He thought he had caught a large fish, and he felt very pleased. But a moment afterwards, seeing that instead of a fish he only had in his nets the carcase of an ass, he was much disappointed.

Vexed with having such a bad haul, when he had mended his nets, which the carcase of the ass had broken in several places, he threw them a second time. In drawing them in, he again felt a great weight, so that he thought they were full of fish. But he only found a large basket full of rubbish. He was much annoyed.

'O Fortune,' he cried, 'do not trifle thus with me, a poor fisherman, who can hardly support his family!'

So saying, he threw away the rubbish, and after having washed his nets clean of the dirt, he threw them for the third time. But he only drew in stones, shells, and mud. He was almost in despair.

Then he threw his nets for the fourth time. When he thought he had a fish, he drew them in with a great deal of trouble. There was no fish however, but he found a yellow pot, which by its weight seemed full of something, and he noticed that it was fastened and sealed with lead, with the impression of a seal.

He was delighted. 'I will sell it to the founder,' he said; 'with the money I shall get for it, I shall buy a measure of wheat.'

He examined the jar on all sides; he shook it to see if it would rattle. But he heard nothing, and so, judging from the impression of the seal and the lid, he thought there must be something precious inside.

To find out, he took his knife, and with a little trouble he opened it. He turned it upside down, but nothing came out, which surprised him very much. He set it in front of him, and whilst he was looking at it attentively, such a thick smoke came out that he had to step back a pace or two.

This smoke rose up to the clouds and, stretching over the sea and the shore, formed a thick mist, which caused the fisherman much astonishment. When all the smoke was out of the jar, it gathered itself together and became a thick mass in which appeared a jinn, twice as large as the largest giant. When he saw such a terrible-looking monster, the fisherman would like to have run away, but he trembled so with fright that he could not move a step.

'Great king of the jinns,' cried the monster, 'I will never again disobey you!'

At these words the fisherman took courage. 'What is this you are saying, great jinn? Tell me your history and how you came to be shut up in that vase.'

At this, the jinn looked at the fisherman haughtily. 'Speak to me more civilly,' he said, 'before I kill you.'

'Alas! Why should you kill me?' cried the fisherman. 'I have just freed you; have you already forgotten that?'

'No,' answered the jinn; 'but that will not prevent me from killing you; and I am only going to grant you one favour, and that is to choose the manner of your death.'

'But what have I done to you?' asked the fisherman.

'I cannot treat you in any other way,' said the jinn, 'and if you would know why, listen to my story.

'I rebelled against the king of the jinns. To punish me, he shut me up in this vase of copper, and he put on the leaden cover his seal, which is enchantment enough to prevent my coming out. Then he had the vase thrown into the sea. During the first period of my captivity, I vowed that if anyone should free me before a hundred years were passed, I would make him rich even after his death. But that century passed, and no one freed me. In the second century, I vowed that I would give all the treasures in the world to my deliverer; but he never came.

'In the third, I promised to make him a king, to be always near him, and to grant him three wishes every day; but that century passed away as the other two had done, and I remained in the same plight. At last, I grew angry at being captive for so long, and I vowed that if anyone would release me, I would kill him at once, and would only allow him to choose in what manner he should die. So, you see, as you have freed me today, choose in what way you will die.'

The fisherman was very unhappy. 'What an unlucky man I am to have freed you! I implore you to spare my life.'

'I have told you,' said the jinn, 'that it is impossible. Choose quickly; you are wasting time.'

The fisherman began to devise a plot. 'Since I must die,' he said, 'before I choose the manner of my death, I conjure you on your honour to tell me if you really were in that vase?'

'Yes, I was,' answered the jinn.

'I really cannot believe it,' said the fisherman. 'That vase could not contain one of your feet even, and how could your whole body go in? I cannot believe it unless I see you do the thing.'

Then the jinn began to change himself into smoke, which, as before, spread over the sea and the shore, and which, then collecting itself together, began to go back into the vase slowly and evenly till there was nothing left outside. Then a voice came from the vase which said to the fisherman, 'Well, unbelieving fisherman, here I am in the vase; do you believe me now?'

The fisherman, instead of answering, took the lid of lead and shut it down quickly on the vase.

'Now, O jinn,' he cried, 'ask pardon of me, and choose by what death you will die! But no, it will be better if I throw you into the sea whence I drew you out, and I will build a house on the shore to warn fishermen who come to cast their nets here, against fishing up such a wicked genius as you are, who vows to kill the man who frees you.'

At these words, the jinn did all he could to get out, but he could not, because of the enchantment of the lid.

From: One Thousand and One Nights

How Footbinding Started

IN THE VERY beginning of all things, when the gods were creating the world, at last the time came to separate the earth from the heavens.

This was hard work, and if it had not been for the coolness and skill of a young goddess, all would have failed. This goddess was named Lu-o. She had been idly watching the growth of the planet when, to her horror, she saw the newly made ball slipping slowly from its place.

In another second, it would have shot down into the bottomless pit. Quick as a flash, Lu-o stopped it with her magic wand and held it firmly until the chief god came dashing up to the rescue.

But this was not all. When men and women were put on the earth, Lu-o helped them greatly by setting an example of purity and kindness. Everyone loved her and pointed her out as the one who was always willing to do a good deed.

After she had left the world and gone into the land of the gods, beautiful statues of her were set up in many temples to keep her image always before the eyes of sinful people. The greatest of these was in the capital city. Thus, when sorrowful women wished to offer up their prayers to some virtuous goddess, they would go to a temple of Lu-o and pour out their hearts before her shrine.

At one time, the wicked Chow-sin, last ruler of the Yins, went to pray in the city Temple. There, his royal eyes were captivated by the sight of a wonderful face, the beauty of which was so great that he fell in love with it at once, telling his ministers that he wished he might take this goddess, who was no other than Lu-o, for one of his wives.

Now, Lu-o was terribly angry that an earthly prince should dare to make such a remark about her. Then and there, she determined to punish the emperor. Calling her assistant spirits, she told them of Chow-sin's insult. Of all her servants, the most cunning was one whom we shall call Fox Sprite, because he really belonged to the fox family. Lu-o ordered Fox Sprite to spare himself no trouble in making the wicked ruler suffer for his impudence.

For many days, try as he would, Chow-sin, the great Son of Heaven, could not forget the face he had seen in the temple.

'He is stark mad,' laughed his courtiers behind his back, 'to fall in love with a statue.'

'I must find a woman just like her,' said the emperor, 'and take her to wife.'

'Why not, most Mighty One,' suggested a favourite adviser, 'send forth a command throughout the length and breadth of your Empire, that no maiden shall be taken in marriage until you have chosen yourself a wife whose beauty shall equal that of Lu-o?'

Chow-sin was pleased with this suggestion and doubtless would have followed it had not his prime minister begged him to postpone issuing the order.

'Your Imperial Highness,' began the official, 'since you have been pleased once or twice to follow my counsel, I beg of you to give ear now to what I say.'

'Speak, and your words shall have my best attention,' replied Chow-sin, with a gracious wave of the hand.

'Know then, Great One, that in the southern part of your realm, there dwells a viceroy whose bravery has made him famous in battle.'

'Are you speaking of Su-nan?' questioned Chow-sin, frowning, for this Su-nan had once been a rebel.

'None other, mighty Son of Heaven. Famous is he as a soldier, but his name is now even greater in that he is the father of the most beautiful girl in all China. This lovely flower that has bloomed of late within his household is still unmarried. Why not order her father to bring her to the palace that you may wed her and place her in your royal dwelling?'

'And are you sure of this wondrous beauty you describe so prettily?' asked the ruler, a smile of pleasure lighting up his face.

'So sure that I will stake my head on your being satisfied.'

'Enough! I command you at once to summon the viceroy and his daughter. Add the imperial seal to the message.'

The prime minister smilingly departed to give the order. In his heart, he was more than delighted that the emperor had accepted his suggestion, for Su-nan, the viceroy, had long been his chief enemy, and he planned in this way to overthrow him.

The viceroy, as he knew, was a man of iron. He would certainly not feel honoured at the thought of having his daughter enter the Imperial palace as a secondary wife. Doubtless, he would refuse to obey the order and would thus bring about his own immediate downfall.

Nor was the prime minister mistaken.

When Su-nan received the imperial message, his heart was hot with anger against his sovereign. To be robbed of his lovely Ta-ki, even by the throne, was, in his eyes, a terrible disgrace. Could he have been sure that she would be made Empress it might have been different, but with so many others sharing Chow-sin's favour, her promotion to first place in the Great One's household was by no means certain. Besides, she was Su-nan's favourite child, and the old man could not bear the thought of separation from her. Rather would he give up his life than let her go to this cruel ruler.

'No, you shall not do it,' said he to Ta-ki, 'not though I must die to save you.'

The beautiful girl listened to her father's words, in tears. Throwing herself at his feet, she thanked him for his mercy and promised to love him more fondly than ever. She told him that her vanity had not been flattered by what most girls might have thought an honour, that she would rather have the love of one good man like her father than share with others the affections of a king.

After listening to his daughter, the viceroy sent a respectful answer to the palace, thanking the emperor for his favour, but saying he could not give up Ta-ki.

'She is unworthy of the honour you purpose doing her,' he said, in conclusion, 'for, having been the apple of her father's eye, she would not be happy to share even your most august favour with the many others you have chosen.'

When the emperor learned of Su-nan's reply, he could hardly believe his ears. To have his command thus disobeyed was an unheard-of crime. Never before had a subject of the Middle kingdom offered such an insult to a ruler. Boiling with rage, he ordered his prime minister to send forth an army that would bring the viceroy to his senses.

'Tell him if he disobeys, that he and his family – together with all they possess – shall be destroyed.'

Delighted at the success of his plot against Su-nan, the prime minister sent a regiment of soldiers to bring the rebel to terms. In the meantime, the friends of the daring viceroy had not been idle. Hearing of the danger threatening their ruler, who had become a general favourite, hundreds of men offered him their aid against the army of Chow-sin.

Thus, when the emperor's banners were seen approaching and the war drums were heard rolling in the distance, the rebels, with a great shout, dashed forth to do battle for their leader. In the fight that took place, the Imperial soldiers were forced to run.

When the emperor heard of this defeat, he was hot with anger. He called together his advisers and commanded that an army, double the size of the first one, should be sent to Su-nan's country to destroy the fields and villages of the people who had risen up against him.

'Spare not one of them,' he shouted, 'for they are traitors to the Dragon Throne.'

Once more, the viceroy's friends resolved to support him, even to the death. Ta-ki, his daughter, went apart from the other members of the family, weeping most bitterly that she had brought such sorrow upon them.

'Rather would I go into the palace and be the lowest among Chow-sin's women than to be the cause of all this grief,' she cried, in desperation.

But her father soothed her, saying, 'Be of good cheer, Ta-ki. The emperor's army, though it be twice as large as mine, shall not overcome us. Right is on our side. The gods of battle will help those who fight for justice.'

One week later, a second battle was fought, and the struggle was so close that none could foresee the result. The Imperial army was commanded by the oldest nobles in the kingdom, those most skilled in warfare, while the viceroy's men were young and poorly drilled. Moreover, the members of the Dragon Army had been promised double pay if they should accomplish the wishes of their sovereign, while Su-nan's soldiers knew only too well that they would be put to the sword if they should be defeated.

Just as the clash of arms was at its highest, the sound of gongs was heard upon a distant hill. The government troops were amazed at seeing fresh companies marching to the rescue of their foe. With a wild cry of disappointment, they turned and fled from the field. These unexpected reinforcements turned out to be women whom Ta-ki had persuaded to dress up as soldiers and go with her for the purpose of frightening the enemy. Thus, for a second time was Su-nan victorious.

During the following year, several battles occurred that counted for little, except that in each of them many of Su-nan's followers were killed. At last one of the viceroy's best friends came to him, saying, 'Noble lord, it is useless to continue the struggle. I fear you must give up the fight.

You have lost more than half your supporters; the remaining bowmen are either sick or wounded and can be of little use. The emperor, moreover, is even now raising a new army from the distant provinces, and will soon send against us a force ten times as great as any we have yet seen. There being no hope of victory, further fighting would be folly. Lead, therefore, your daughter to the palace. Throw yourself upon the mercy of the throne. You must accept cheerfully the fate the gods have suffered you to bear.'

Ta-ki, chancing to overhear this conversation, rushed in and begged her father to hold out no longer, but to deliver her up to the greed of the wicked Chow-sin.

With a sigh, the viceroy yielded to their wishes. The next day, he despatched a messenger to the emperor, promising to bring Ta-ki at once to the capital.

Now we must not forget Fox Sprite, the demon, who had been commanded by the good goddess Lu-o to bring a dreadful punishment upon the emperor. Through all the years of strife between Chow-sin and the rebels, Fox Sprite had been waiting patiently for his chance. He knew well that someday, sooner or later, there would come an hour when Chow-sin would be at his mercy.

When the time came, therefore, for Ta-ki to go to the palace, Fox Sprite felt that at last his chance had come. The beautiful maiden for whom Chow-sin had given up so many hundreds of his soldiers would clearly have great power over the emperor. She must be made to help in the punishment of her wicked husband. So Fox Sprite made himself invisible and travelled with the viceroy's party as it went from central China to the capital.

On the last night of their journey, Su-nan and his daughter stopped for rest and food at a large inn. No sooner had the girl gone to her room for the night than Fox Sprite followed her. Then he made himself visible. At first, she was frightened to see so strange a being in her room, but when Fox Sprite told her he was a servant of the great goddess, Lu-o, she was comforted, for she knew that Lu-o was the friend of women and children.

'But how can I help to punish the emperor?' she faltered, when the sprite told her he wanted her assistance. 'I am but a helpless girl,' and here she began to cry.

'Dry your tears,' he said soothingly. 'It will be very easy. Only let me take your form for a little. When I am the emperor's wife,' laughing, 'I shall find a way to punish him, for no one can give a man more pain that his wife can, if she desires to do so. You know, I am a servant of Lu-o and can do anything I wish.'

'But the emperor won't have a fox for a wife,' she sobbed.

'Though I am still a fox I shall look like the beautiful Ta-ki. Make your heart easy. He will never know.'

'Oh, I see,' she smiled, 'you will put your spirit into my body and you will look just like me, though you really won't be me. But what will become of the real me? Shall I have to be a fox and look like you?'

'No, not unless you want to. I will make you invisible, and you can be ready to go back into your own body when I have got rid of the emperor.'

'Very well,' replied the girl, somewhat relieved by his explanation, 'but try not to be too long about it, because I don't like the idea of somebody else walking about in my body.'

So Fox Sprite caused his own spirit to enter the girl's body, and no one could have told by her outward appearance that any change had taken place. The beautiful girl was now in reality the sly Fox Sprite, but in one way only did she look like a fox. When the fox-spirit entered her body, her feet suddenly shrivelled up and became very similar in shape and size to the feet of the animal who had her in his power. When the fox noticed this, at first he was somewhat annoyed, but, feeling that no one else would know, he did not take the trouble to change the fox feet back to human form.

On the following morning, when the viceroy called his daughter for the last stage of their journey, he greeted Fox Sprite without suspecting that anything unusual had happened since he had last seen Ta-ki. So well did this crafty spirit perform his part, that the father was completely deceived, by look, by voice and by gesture.

The next day, the travellers arrived at the capital and Su-nan presented himself before Chow-sin, the emperor, leading Fox Sprite with him. Of course, the crafty fox with all his magic powers was soon able to gain the mastery over the wicked ruler. The Great One pardoned Su-nan, although he had fully intended to put him to death as a rebel.

Now the chance for which Fox Sprite had been waiting had come. He began at once, causing the emperor to do many deeds of violence. The people had already begun to dislike Chow-sin, and soon he became hateful in their sight.

Many of the leading members of the court were put to death unjustly. Horrible tortures were devised for punishing those who did not find favour with the crown. At last, there was open talk of a rebellion. Of course, all these things delighted the wily fox, for he saw that, sooner or later, the Son of Heaven would be turned out of the palace, and he knew that then his work for the goddess Lu-o would be finished.

Besides worming his way into the heart of the emperor, the fox became a general favourite with the ladies of the palace. These women saw in Chow-sin's latest wife the most beautiful woman who had ever lived in the royal harem. One would think that this beauty might have caused them to hate Fox Sprite, but such was not the case. They admired the plumpness of Fox Sprite's body, the fairness of Fox Sprite's complexion, the fire in Fox Sprite's eyes, but most of all they wondered at the smallness of Fox Sprite's feet, for, you remember, the supposed Ta-ki now had fox's feet instead of those of human shape.

Thus, small feet became the fashion among women. All the court ladies, old and young, beautiful and ugly, began thinking of plans for making their own feet as tiny as those of Fox Sprite. In this way, they thought to increase their chances of finding favour with the emperor.

Gradually, people outside the palace began to hear of this absurd fashion. Mothers bound the feet of their little girls in such a manner as to stop their growth. The bones of the toes were bent backwards and broken, so eager were the elders to have their daughters grow up into tiny-footed maidens.

Thus, for several years of their girlhood the little ones were compelled to endure the most severe tortures. It was not long before the new fashion took firm root in China. It became almost impossible for parents to get husbands for their daughters unless the girls had suffered the severe pains of foot-binding. And even to this day, we find that many of the people are still under the influence of Fox Sprite's magic, and believe that a tiny, misshapen foot is more beautiful than a natural one.

But let us return to the story of Fox Sprite and the wicked emperor. For a number of years, matters grew continually worse in the country. At last, the people rose in a body against the ruler. A great battle was fought. The wicked Chow-sin was overthrown and put to death by means of those very instruments of torture he had used so often against his subjects. By this time, it had become known to all the lords and noblemen that the emperor's favourite had been the main cause of their ruler's wickedness; hence they demanded the death of Fox Sprite. But no one wished to kill so lovely a creature. Every one appointed refused to do the deed.

Finally, a grey-headed member of the court allowed himself to be blindfolded. With a sharp sword, he pierced the body of Fox Sprite to the heart. Those standing near covered their eyes with their hands, for they could not bear to see so wonderful a woman die.

Suddenly, as they looked up, they saw a sight so strange that all were filled with amazement. Instead of falling to the ground, the graceful form swayed backward and forward for a moment, when all at once there seemed to spring from her side a huge mountain fox. The animal glanced around him, then, with a cry of fear, dashing past officials, courtiers and soldiers, he rushed through the gate of the enclosure.

'A fox!' cried the people, full of wonder.

At that moment, Ta-ki fell in a swoon upon the floor. When they picked her up, thinking, of course, that she had died from the sword thrust, they could find no blood on her body, and, on looking more closely, they saw that there was not even the slightest wound.

'Marvel of marvels!' they all shouted. 'The gods have shielded her!'

Just then Ta-ki opened her eyes and looked about her. 'Where am I?' she asked, in faint voice. 'Pray tell me what has happened.'

Then they told her what they had seen, and at last it was plain to the beautiful woman that, after all these years, Fox Sprite had left her body. She was herself once more. For a long time, she could not make the people believe her story; they all said that she must have lost her mind; that the gods had saved her life, but had punished her for her wickedness by taking away her reason.

But that night, when her maids were undressing her in the palace, they saw her feet, which had once more become their natural size, and then they knew she had been telling the truth.

From: A Chinese Wonder Book

Dinewan the Emu, &

Goomblegubbon the Bustard

Dinewan the emu, being the largest bird, was acknowledged as king by the other birds. The Goomblegubbons, the bustards, were jealous of the Dinewans. Particularly was Goomblegubbon, the mother, jealous of the Diriewan mother. She would watch with envy the high flight of the Dinewans and their swift running.

And she always fancied that the Dinewan mother flaunted her superiority in her face, for whenever Dinewan alighted near Goomblegubbon after a long, high flight, she would flap her big wings and begin booing in her pride, not the loud booing of the male bird, but a little, triumphant, satisfied booing noise of her own, which never failed to irritate Goomblegubbon when she heard it.

Goomblegubbon used to wonder how she could put an end to Dinewan's supremacy. She decided that she would only be able to do so by injuring her wings and checking her power of flight. But the question that troubled her was how to effect this end. She knew she would gain nothing by having a quarrel with Dinewan and fighting her, for no Goomblegubbon would stand any chance against a

Dinewan. There was evidently nothing to be gained by an open fight. She would have to affect her end by cunning.

One day, when Goomblegubbon saw in the distance Dinewan coming towards her, she squatted down and doubled in her wings in such a way as to look as if she had none. After Dinewan had been talking to her for some time, Goomblegubbon said: 'Why do you not imitate me and do without wings? Every bird flies. The Dinewans, to be the king of birds, should do without wings. When all the birds see that I can do without wings, they will think I am the cleverest bird and they will make a Goomblegubbon king.'

'But you have wings,' said Dinewan.

'No, I have no wings.' And indeed she looked as if her words were true, so well were her wings hidden, as she squatted in the grass. Dinewan went away after a while, and thought much of what she had heard. She talked it all over with her mate, who was as disturbed as she was. They made up their minds that it would never do to let the Goomblegubbons reign in their stead, even if they had to lose their wings to save their kingship.

At length, they decided on the sacrifice of their wings. The Dinewan mother showed the example by persuading her mate to cut off hers with a combo or stone tomahawk, and then she did the same to his. As soon as the operations were over, the Dinewan mother lost no time in letting Goomblegubbon know what they had done. She ran swiftly down to the plain on which she had left Goomblegubbon, and, finding her still squatting there, she said: 'See, I have followed your example. I have now no wings. They are cut off.'

'Ha! Ha! Ha!' laughed Goomblegubbon, jumping up and dancing round with joy at the success of her plot. As she danced round, she spread out her wings, flapped them, and said: 'I have taken you in, old stumpy wings. I have my wings yet. You are fine birds, you Dinewans, to be chosen kings, when you are so easily taken in. Ha! Ha! Ha!'

And, laughing derisively, Goomblegubbon flapped her wings right in front of Dinewan, who rushed towards her to chastise her treachery. But Goomblegubbon flew away, and, alas! The now wingless Dinewan could not follow her.

Brooding over her wrongs, Dinewan walked away, vowing she would be revenged. But how? That was the question which she and her mate failed to answer for some time. At length, the Dinewan mother thought of a plan and prepared at once to execute it. She hid all her young Dinewans but two under a big salt bush. Then, she walked off to Goomblegubbons' plain with the two young ones following her. As she walked off the morilla ridge – where her home was – onto the plain, she saw Goomblegubbon out feeding with her twelve young ones.

After exchanging a few remarks in a friendly manner with Goomblegubbon, she said to her, 'Why do you not imitate me and only have two children? Twelve are too many to feed. If you keep so many, they will never grow big birds like the Dinewans. The food that would make big birds of two would only starve twelve.'

Goomblegubbon said nothing, but she thought it might be so. It was impossible to deny that the young Dinewans were much bigger than the young Goomblegubbons, and, discontentedly, Goomblegubbon walked away, wondering whether the smallness of her young ones was owing to the number of them being so much greater than that of the Dinewans. It would be grand, she thought, to grow as big as the Dinewans. But she remembered the trick she had played on Dinewan, and she thought that perhaps she was being fooled in her turn.

She looked back to where the Dinewans fed, and as she saw how much bigger the two young ones were than any of hers, once more mad envy of Dinewan possessed her. She determined she would not be outdone. Rather would she kill all her young ones but two. She said, 'The Dinewans shall not be the king birds of the plains. The Goomblegubbons shall replace them. They shall grow as big as the Dinewans, and shall keep their wings and fly, which now the Dinewans cannot do.'

And straightway, Goomblegubbon killed all her young ones but two. Then back she came to where the Dinewans were still feeding. When Dinewan saw her coming and noticed she had only two young ones with her, she called out: 'Where are all your young ones?'

Goomblegubbon answered, 'I have killed them, and have only two left. Those will have plenty to eat now, and will soon grow as big as your young ones.'

'You cruel mother to kill your children. You greedy mother. Why, I have twelve children and I find food for them all. I would not kill one for anything, not even if by so doing I could get back my wings. There is plenty for all. Look at the emu bush, how it covers itself with berries to feed my big family. See how the grasshoppers come hopping round, so that we can catch them and fatten on them.'

'But you have only two children.'

'I have twelve. I will go and bring them to show you.'

Dinewan ran off to her salt bush, where she had hidden her ten young ones. Soon, she was to be seen coming back. Running with her neck stretched forward, her head thrown back with pride, and the feathers of her boobootella swinging as she ran, booming out the while her queer throat noise, the Dinewan song of joy, the pretty, soft-looking little ones with their zebra-striped skins running beside her whistling their baby Dinewan note.

When Dinewan reached the place where Goomblegubbon was, she stopped her booing and said in a solemn tone, 'Now you see my words are true; I have twelve young ones, as I said. You can gaze at my loved ones and think of your poor murdered children. And while you do so, I will tell you the fate of your descendants forever. By trickery and deceit, you lost the Dinewans their wings, and now for evermore, as long as a Dinewan has no wings, so long shall a Goomblegubbon lay only two eggs and have only two young ones. We are quits now. You have your wings and I my children.'

And ever since that time, a Dinewan, or emu, has had no wings, and a Goomblegubbon, or bustard of the plains, has laid only two eggs in a season.

From: Australian Legendary Tales

The Lassie & Her Godmother

ONCE ON A time, a poor couple lived far, far away in a great wood. The wife was brought to bed, and had a pretty girl, but they were so poor they did not know how to get the babe christened, for they had no money to pay the parson's fees.

So one day, the father went out to see if he could find anyone who was willing to stand for the child and pay the fees; but though he walked about the whole day from one house to another, and though all said they were willing enough to stand, no one thought himself bound to pay the fees.

Now, when he was going home again, a lovely lady met him, dressed so fine, and she looked so thoroughly good and kind; she offered to get the babe christened, but after that, she said, she must keep it for her own. The husband answered he must first ask his wife what she wished to do; but when he got home and told his story, the wife said, right out, 'No!'

Next day, the man went out again, but no one would stand if they had to pay the fees; and though he begged and prayed, he could get no help. And again as he went home, towards evening the same lovely lady met him, who looked so sweet and good, and she made him the same offer. So he told his wife again how he had fared, and this time she said, if he couldn't get any one to stand for his babe next day, they must just let the lady have her way, since she seemed so kind and good.

The third day, the man went about, but he couldn't get any one to stand; and so when, towards evening, he met the kind lady again, he gave his word she should have the babe if she would only get it christened at the font. So next morning, she came to the place where the man lived, followed by two men to stand godfathers, took the babe and carried it to church, and there it was christened. After that she took it to her own house, and there the little girl lived with her several years, and her foster mother was always kind and friendly to her.

Now, when the Lassie had grown to be big enough to know right and wrong, her foster mother got ready to go on a journey. 'You have my leave,' she said, 'to go all over the house, except those rooms which I show you;' and when she had said that, away she went.

But the Lassie could not forbear just to open one of the doors a little bit, when – Pop! ut flew a Star.

When her foster mother came back, she was very vexed to find that the star had flown out, and she got very angry with her foster daughter, and threatened to send her away; but the child cried and begged so hard that she got leave to stay.

Now, after a while, the foster mother had to go on another journey; and, before she went, she forbade the Lassie to go into those two rooms into which she had never been. She promised to beware; but when she was left alone, she began to think and to wonder what there could be in the second room, and at last she could not help setting the door a little ajar, just to peep in, when – Pop! Out flew the Moon.

When her foster mother came home and found the moon let out, she was very downcast, and said to the Lassie she must go away, she could not stay with her any longer. But the Lassie wept so bitterly, and prayed so heartily for forgiveness, that this time, too, she got leave to stay.

Sometime after, the foster mother had to go away again, and she charged the Lassie, who by this time was half grown up, most earnestly that she mustn't try to go into, or to peep into, the third room. But when her foster mother had been gone some time, and the Lassie was weary of walking about alone, all at once she thought, 'Dear me, what fun it would be just to peep a little into that third room.'

Then, she thought she mustn't do it for her foster-mother's sake; but when the bad thought came the second time, she could hold out no longer; come what might, she must and would look into the room; so she just opened the door a tiny bit, when – POP! Out flew the sun.

But when her foster mother came back and saw that the sun had flown away, she was cut to the heart, and said, 'Now, there was no help for it, the Lassie must and should go away; she couldn't hear of her staying any longer.'

Now the Lassie cried her eyes out, and begged and prayed so prettily; but it was all no good.

'Nay! But I must punish you!' said her foster mother; 'but you may have your choice, either to be the loveliest woman in the world, and not to be able to speak, or to keep your speech, and to be the ugliest of all women; but away from me you must go.'

And the Lassie said, 'I would sooner be lovely.'

So she became all at once wondrous fair; but from that day forth she was dumb.

So, when she went away from her foster mother, she walked and wandered through a great, great wood; but the farther she went, the farther off the end seemed to be. So, when the evening came on, she climbed up into a tall tree, which grew over a spring, and there she made herself up to sleep that night.

Close by lay a castle, and from that castle came early every morning a maid to draw water to make the prince's tea, from the spring over which the Lassie was sitting. So the maid looked down into the spring, saw the lovely face in the water, and thought it was her own; then she flung away the pitcher, and ran home; and, when she got there, she tossed up her head and said, 'If I'm so pretty, I'm far too good to go and fetch water.'

So another maid had to go for the water, but the same thing happened to her; she went back and said she was far too pretty and too good to fetch water from the spring for the prince.

Then the prince went himself, for he had a mind to see what all this could mean. So, when he reached the spring, he too saw the image in the water; but he looked up at once, and became aware of the lovely Lassie who sat there up in the tree. Then, he coaxed her down and took her home; and at last made up his mind to have her for his queen, because she was so lovely; but his mother, who was still alive, was against it.

'She can't speak,' she said, 'and maybe she's a wicked witch.'

But the prince could not be content till he got her. So after they had lived together a while, the Lassie was to have a child, and when the child came to be born, the prince set a strong watch about her; but at the birth one and all fell into a deep sleep, and her foster mother came, cut the babe on its little finger, and smeared the queen's mouth with the blood; and said: 'Now you shall be as grieved as I was when you let out the star;' and with these words she carried off the babe.

But when those who were on the watch woke, they thought the queen had eaten her own child, and the old queen was all for burning her alive, but the prince was so fond of her that at last, he begged her off, but he had hard work to set her free.

So the next time the young queen was to have a child, twice as strong a watch was set as the first time, but the same thing happened over again, only this time her foster mother said: 'Now you shall be as grieved as I was when you let the moon out.'

And the queen begged and prayed, and wept; for when her foster mother was there, she could speak – but it was all no good.

And now, the old queen said she must be burnt, but the prince found means to beg her off. But when the third child was to be born, a watch was set three times as strong as the first, but just the same thing happened. Her foster mother came while the watch slept, took the babe, and cut its little finger, and smeared the queen's mouth with the blood, telling her now she should be as grieved as she had been when the Lassie let out the sun.

And now, the prince could not save her any longer. She must and should be burnt. But just as they were leading her to the stake, all at once they saw her foster mother, who came with all three children – two she led by the hand, and the third she had on her arm; and so she went up to the young queen and said: 'Here are your children; now you shall have them again. I am the Virgin Mary, and so grieved as you have been, so grieved was I when you let out sun, and moon, and star. Now you have been punished for what you did, and henceforth you shall have your speech.'

How glad the queen and prince now were, all may easily think, but no one can tell. After that they were always happy; and from that day even the prince's mother was very fond of the young queen.

From: East of the Sun & West of the Moon

Silver Bells

IT WAS IN a lovely pine-wood that little Mirabella wandered lonely and hungry. The sand under her feet was very cool, and the tufted pine-trees sheltered her from the fierce rays of the sun.

Through an avenue of tall but bare pine-trees she could see the big sea, which she looked upon for the first time. Faint and hungry as she was, she could not help wishing to be nearer the waves; but she recollected what her father had once told her, that little children should be careful not to go too near the sea when they are alone.

Her father, however, was dead. He was king of the Silver Isles, and for his goodness had been loved by all his subjects. Mirabella was his only child; and her mother having married again, she wanted to get rid of Mirabella, so that her little boy Gliglu might inherit the crown. So she ordered one of her servants to lead Mirabella into the pine-wood far away and leave her there, hoping the wolves would find her and eat her.

When Mirabella was born, her aunt, who was a fairy, gave her a silver bell, which she tied around the child's neck with a fairy chain that could not be broken. In vain did her mother try to take it from her; no scissors could cut through it, and her strength could not break it, so that wherever Mirabella went the silver bell tinkled merrily.

Now, it so happened that on the second night on which she was out the silver bell tinkled so loudly, that a wolf who happened to be near, hearing it, approached her and said –

'Silver bell, silver bell, do not fear;
To obey you, Mirabella, I am here.'

At first the little girl was very much afraid, because she had heard of the cruelty of wolves; but when he repeated the words, she said, 'Dear Mr. Wolf, if you would be so kind as to bring me my mamma, I would be so obliged.'

Off ran the wolf without saying another word, and Mirabella commenced jumping for joy, causing her silver bell to tinkle more than ever. A fox, hearing it, came up to her and said,

'Silver bell, silver bell, do not fear;
To obey you, Mirabella, I am here.'

Then she said, 'Oh, dear Mr. Fox, I am so hungry! I wish you would bring me something to eat.'

Off went the fox, and in a short time he returned with a roast fowl, bread, a plate, knife, and fork, all nicely placed in a basket. On the top of these things was a clean white cloth, which she spread on the ground, and on which she placed her dinner. She was indeed thankful to the fox for his kindness, and patted his head, which made him wag his thick brush. She enjoyed her dinner very much; but she was very thirsty.

She thought she would try tinkling her bell, and no sooner had she done so than she heard the tinkling of another bell in the distance, coming nearer and nearer to her. She stood on tiptoe, and she saw a stream of water flowing towards her, on which floated a pretty canoe.

When it got up to her it stopped, and inside the canoe was a silver mug; but on the bows of the canoe was hanging a silver bell just like her own.

> 'Silver bell, silver bell, do not fear;
> When thy mother comes, step in here.'

So sang the canoe; but she could not understand why she should get into the canoe if her mother came, because she loved her mother, and thought her mother loved her. Anyhow, she took hold of the mug, and, filling it with water, drank it up. Water, which is always the most refreshing of all drinks, was what the tired little girl most needed, and as her father had brought her up very carefully and properly, she had never tasted anything stronger; but her thirst made her enjoy the water more than she ever had.

Suddenly, she heard someone screaming for help, and the screams came nearer and nearer to her. She turned round and saw the wolf bearing her mother on his back, and however much she tried to get off she could not, because the wolf threatened to bite her.

Springing up to Mirabella's side, the wolf said,

'Silver bell, silver bell, do not fear;
To obey you, Mirabella, I am here.'

The wicked mother now jumped off his back, and commenced scolding Mirabella for having sent for her. She said that as soon as she got back to the palace she would make a law that all the wolves should be killed, and that if Mirabella ever dared return she should be smothered. The poor little girl felt very miserable, and was afraid that her mother might kill her, so she stepped into the canoe, and said,

'Bear me where my father dwells,
Tinkle, tinkle, silver bells.'

The stream continued to flow, and as the canoe moved on, she saw her mother turned into a cork-tree, and she bid goodbye to the wolf and the fox. On sped the boat, and it soon neared the big sea; but Mirabella felt no fear, for the stream struck out across the ocean, and the waves did not come near her.

For three days and nights, the silver bells tinkled and the canoe sped on; and when the morning of the fourth day came, she saw that they were approaching a beautiful island, on which were growing many palm trees, which are called sacred palms. The grass was far greener than any she had ever seen, for the sun was more brilliant, but not so fierce, and when the canoe touched the shore – oh, joy! – she saw her dear father.

'Silver bell, silver bell, do not fear;
To protect thee, Mirabella, I am here.'

She was so pleased to see her father again and to hear him
speak. It was so nice to be loved, to be cared for, to be spoken
kindly to. Everything seemed to welcome her; the boughs
of the sacred palms waved in the summer breeze, and the
humming-birds, flitting about, seemed like precious stones
set in a glorious blaze of light. Her father was not changed
very much; he looked somewhat younger and stronger, and
as he lifted her in his arms his face seemed handsomer and
his voice more welcome. She felt no pang of sorrow, she had
no fears, for she was in her father's arms, to which the fairy
silver bells had led her.

Farther up in the island, she saw groups of other children
running to meet her, all with silver bells around their necks;
and some there were among them whom she had known in
the Silver Islands. These had been playmates of hers, but
had left before her.

So periods of light sped on, in which joy was her
companion, when, looking into a deep but very clear pond,
she saw a gnarled cork-tree, which seemed to have been
struck by lightning. Long did she stand there gazing into
it, wondering where she had seen that tree. All at once,
she spied a canoe passing close by the tree, in which stood
a young man, whom she recognized as her step-brother
Gliglu. He seemed to cast a sorrowful look at the tree, and
then she recollected the fate of her mother.

At this moment, her silver bell fell off, and, sinking into the pond, it went down – down, until it reached the tree, and, tinkling, said,

'Take thy shape again, O queen!'

Then, Mirabella saw her mother step into the canoe; and tinkling bells in a short space of time told her that others dear and near to her had arrived, and, running down to the shore, she cried out,

'Silver bells, O mother, wait you here,
Nought but joy with father, nought to fear.'

From: Tales from the Lands of Nuts & Grapes

The She-bear

TRULY THE WISE man said well that a command of gall cannot be obeyed like one of sugar. A man must require just and reasonable things if he would see the scales of obedience properly trimmed.

From orders which are improper springs resistance which is not easily overcome, as happened to the king of Rough-Rock, who, by asking what he ought not of his daughter, caused her to run away from him, at the risk of losing both honour and life.

There lived, it is said, once upon a time a king of Rough-Rock, who had a wife the very mother of beauty, but in the full career of her years, she fell from the horse of health and broke her life. Before the candle of life went out at the auction of her years she called her husband and said to him, 'I know you have always loved me tenderly; show me, therefore, at the close of my days the completion of your love by promising me never to marry again, unless you find a woman as beautiful as I have been, otherwise I leave you my curse, and shall bear you hatred even in the other world.'

The king, who loved his wife beyond measure, hearing this her last wish, burst into tears, and for some time could not answer a single word. At last, when he had done weeping, he said to her, 'Sooner than take another wife may the gout lay hold of me; may I have my head cut off like a mackerel! My dearest love, drive such a thought from your mind; do not believe in dreams, or that I could love any other woman; you were the first new coat of my love, and you shall carry away with you the last rags of my affection.'

As he said these words, the poor young queen, who was at the point of death, turned up her eyes and stretched out her feet. When the king saw her life thus running out, he unstopped the channels of his eyes, and made such a howling and beating and outcry that all the Court came running up, calling on the name of the dear soul, and upbraiding Fortune for taking her from him, and plucking out his beard, he cursed the stars that had sent him such a misfortune.

But bearing in mind the maxim, 'Pain in one's elbow and pain for one's wife are alike hard to bear, but are soon over,' ere the Night had gone forth into the place-of-arms in the sky to muster the bats, he began to count upon his fingers and to reflect thus to himself, 'Here is my wife dead, and I am left a wretched widower, with no hope of seeing anyone but this poor daughter whom she has left me. I must therefore try to discover some means or other of having a son and heir. But where shall I look? Where shall I find a woman equal in beauty to my wife? Everyone appears a witch in comparison with her; where, then, shall I find another with a bit of stick, or seek another with the bell, if Nature made Nardella (may she be in glory), and then broke the mould?

'Alas, in what a labyrinth has she put me, in what a perplexity has the promise I made her left me! But what do

I say? I am running away before I have seen the wolf; let me open my eyes and ears and look about; may there not be some other as beautiful? Is it possible that the world should be lost to me? Is there such a dearth of women, or is the race extinct?'

So saying, he forthwith issued a proclamation and command that all the handsome women in the world should come to the touchstone of beauty, for he would take the most beautiful to wife and endow her with a kingdom. Now, when this news was spread abroad, there was not a woman in the universe who did not come to try her luck – not a witch, however ugly, who stayed behind; for when it is a question of beauty, no scullion-wench will acknowledge herself surpassed; everyone piques herself on being the handsomest; and if the looking glass tells her the truth, she blames the glass for being untrue, and the quicksilver for being put on badly.

When the town was thus filled with women, the king had them all drawn up in a line and he walked up and down from top to bottom, and as he examined and measured each from head to foot, one appeared to him wry-browed, another long-nosed, another broad-mouthed, another thick-lipped, another tall as a maypole, another short and dumpy, another too stout, another too slender; the Spaniard did not please him on account of her dark hair, the Neapolitan was not to his fancy on account of her gait, the German appeared cold and icy, the Frenchwoman frivolous and giddy, the Venetian with her light hair looked like a distaff of flax.

At the end of the end, one for this cause and another for that, he sent them all away, with one hand before and the other behind; and, seeing that so many fair faces were all show and no wool, he turned his thoughts to his own daughter, saying, 'Why do I go seeking the impossible when my daughter Preziosa is formed in the same mould of beauty as her mother? I have this fair face here in my house, and yet go looking for it at the fag-end of the world. She shall marry whom I will, and so I shall have an heir.'

When Preziosa heard this, she retired to her chamber, and bewailing her ill-fortune as if she would not leave a hair upon her head; and, whilst she was lamenting thus, an old woman came to her, who was her confidant. As soon as she saw Preziosa, who seemed to belong more to the other world than to this, and heard the cause of her grief, the old woman said to her, 'Cheer up, my daughter, do not despair; there is a remedy for every evil save death. Now listen; if your father speaks to you thus once again put this bit of wood into your mouth, and instantly you will be changed into a she-bear; then off with you! For in his fright he will let you depart, and go straight to the wood, where Heaven has kept good fortune in store for you since the day you were born, and whenever you wish to appear a woman, as you are and will remain, only take the piece of wood out of your mouth and you will return to your true form.'

Then Preziosa embraced the old woman, and, giving her a good apronful of meal, and ham and bacon, sent her away.

As soon as the sun began to change his quarters, the king ordered the musicians to come and, inviting all his lords and vassals, he held a great feast. And after dancing for five or six hours, they all sat down to table, and ate and drank beyond measure. Then the king asked his courtiers to whom he should marry Preziosa, as she was the picture of his dead wife. But the instant Preziosa heard this, she slipped the bit of wood into her mouth, and took the figure of a terrible she-bear, at the sight of which all present were frightened out of their wits, and ran off as fast as they could scamper.

Meanwhile Preziosa went out and took her way to a wood, where the Shades were holding a consultation how they might do some mischief to the sun at the close of day. And there she stayed, in the pleasant companionship of the other animals, until the son of the king of Running-Water came to hunt in that part of the country, who, at the sight of the bear, had like to have died on the spot.

But when he saw the beast come gently up to him, wagging her tail like a little dog and rubbing her sides against him, he took courage, and patted her, and said, 'Good bear, good bear! there, there! poor beast, poor beast!'

Then he led her home and ordered that she should be taken great care of; and he had her put into a garden close to the royal palace, that he might see her from the window whenever he wished.

One day, when all the people of the house were gone out, and the prince was left alone, he went to the window to look out at the bear; and there he beheld Preziosa, who had taken the piece of wood out of her mouth, combing her golden tresses. At the sight of this beauty, which was beyond the beyonds, he had like to have lost his senses with amazement, and tumbling down the stairs, he ran out into the garden. But Preziosa, who was on the watch and observed him, popped the piece of wood into her mouth, and was instantly changed into a bear again.

When the prince came down and looked about in vain for Preziosa, whom he had seen from the window above, he was so amazed at the trick that a deep melancholy came over him, and in four days he fell sick, crying continually, 'My bear, my bear!'

His mother, hearing him wailing thus, imagined that the bear had done him some hurt, and gave orders that she should be killed. But the servants, enamoured of the tameness of the bear, who made herself beloved by the very stones in the road, took pity on her, and, instead of killing her, they led her to the wood, and told the queen that they had put an end to her.

When this came to the ears of the prince, he acted in a way to pass belief. Ill or well, he jumped out of bed and was going at once to make mincemeat of the servants. But when they told him the truth of the affair, he jumped on horseback, half-dead as he was, and went rambling about and seeking everywhere, until at length he found the bear.

Then he took her home again, and putting her into a chamber, said to her, 'O lovely morsel for a king, who art shut up in this skin! O candle of love, who art enclosed within this hairy lanthorn! Wherefore all this trifling? Do you wish to see me pine and pant, and die by inches? I am wasting away; without hope, and tormented by your beauty. And you see clearly the proof, for I am shrunk two-thirds in size, like wine boiled down, and am nothing but skin and bone, for the fever is double-stitched to my veins.

'So lift up the curtain of this hairy hide, and let me gaze upon the spectacle of your beauty! Raise, O raise the leaves off this basket, and let me get a sight of the fine fruit beneath!

Lift up that curtain, and let my eyes pass in to behold the pomp of wonders! Who has shut up so smooth a creature in a prison woven of hair? Who has locked up so rich a treasure in a leathern chest? Let me behold this display of graces, and take in payment all my love; for nothing else can cure the troubles I endure.'

But when he had said, again and again, this and a great deal more, and still saw that all his words were thrown away, he took to his bed, and had such a desperate fit that the doctors prognosticated badly of his case.

Then his mother, who had no other joy in the world, sat down by his bedside, and said to him, 'My son, whence comes all this grief? What melancholy humour has seized you? You are young, you are loved, you are great, you are rich – what then is it you want, my son? Speak; a bashful beggar carries an empty bag. If you want a wife, only choose, and I will bring the match about; do you take, and I'll pay. Do you not see that your illness is an illness to me? Your pulse beats with fever in your veins, and my heart beats with illness in my brain, for I have no other support of my old age than you. So be cheerful now, and cheer up my heart, and do not see the whole kingdom thrown into mourning, this house into lamentation, and your mother forlorn and heartbroken.'

When the prince heard these words, he said, 'Nothing can console me but the sight of the bear. Therefore, if you wish to see me well again, let her be brought into this chamber; I will have no one else to attend me, and make my bed, and cook for me, but she herself; and you may be sure that this pleasure will make me well in a trice.'

Thereupon his mother, although she thought it ridiculous enough for the bear to act as cook and chambermaid, and feared that her son was not in his right mind, yet, in order to gratify him, had the bear fetched. And when the bear came up to the prince's bed, she raised her paw and felt the patient's pulse, which made the queen laugh outright, for she thought every moment that the bear would scratch his nose.

Then the prince said, 'My dear bear, will you not cook for me, and give me my food, and wait upon me?' and the bear nodded her head, to show that she accepted the office. Then his mother had some fowls brought, and a fire lighted on the hearth in the same chamber, and some water set to boil; whereupon the bear, laying hold on a fowl, scalded and plucked it handily, and drew it, and then stuck one portion of it on the spit, and with the other part she made such a delicious hash that the prince, who could not relish even sugar, licked his fingers at the taste.

And when he had done eating, the bear handed him drink with such grace that the queen was ready to kiss her on the forehead. Thereupon the prince arose, and the bear quickly set about making the bed; and running into the garden, she gathered a clothful of roses and citron-flowers and strewed them over it, so that the queen said the bear was worth her weight in gold, and that her son had good reason to be fond of her.

But when the prince saw these pretty offices, they only added fuel to the fire; and if before he wasted by ounces, he now melted away by pounds, and he said to the queen, 'My lady mother, if I do not give this bear a kiss, the breath will leave my body.'

Whereupon the queen, seeing him fainting away, said, 'Kiss him, kiss him, my beautiful beast! Let me not see my poor son die of longing!'

Then the bear went up to the prince, and taking him by the cheeks, kissed him again and again. Meanwhile (I know not how it was) the piece of wood slipped out of Preziosa's mouth, and she remained in the arms of the prince, the most beautiful creature in the world; and pressing her to his heart, he said, 'I have caught you, my little rogue! You shall not escape from me again without a good reason.'

At these words, Preziosa, adding the colour of modesty to the picture of her natural beauty, said to him, 'I am indeed in your hands – only guard me safely, and marry me when you will.'

Then the queen inquired who the beautiful maiden was, and what had brought her to this savage life; and Preziosa related the whole story of her misfortunes, at which the queen, praising her as a good and virtuous girl, told her son that she was content that Preziosa should be his wife.

Then the prince, who desired nothing else in life, forthwith pledged her his faith; and the mother giving them her blessing, this happy marriage was celebrated with great feasting and illuminations, and Preziosa experienced the truth of the saying that, 'One who acts well may always expect good.'

From: Stories from Pentamerone

How the Monkey Became a Trickster

ONCE UPON A time, there was a beautiful garden in which grew all sorts of fruits. Many beasts lived in the garden and they were permitted to eat of the fruits whenever they wished. But they were asked to observe one rule.

They must make a low, polite bow to the fruit tree, call it by its name, and say, 'Please give me a taste of your fruit.'

They had to be very careful to remember the tree's correct name and not to forget to say 'please.' It was also very important that they should remember not to be greedy. They must always leave plenty of fruit for the other beasts who might pass that way, and plenty to adorn the tree itself and to furnish seed so that other trees might grow.

If they wished to eat figs they had to say, 'O, fig tree, O, fig tree, please give me a taste of your fruit;' or, if they wished to eat oranges they had to say, 'O, orange tree, O, orange tree, please give me a taste of your fruit.'

In one corner of the garden grew the most splendid tree of all. It was tall and beautiful and the rosy-cheeked fruit upon its wide spreading branches looked wonderfully tempting.

No beast had ever tasted of that fruit, for no beast could ever remember its name.

In a tiny house near the edge of the garden dwelt a little old woman who knew the names of all the fruit trees which grew in the garden. The beasts often went to her and asked the name of the wonderful fruit tree, but the tree was so far distant from the tiny house of the little old woman that no beast could ever remember the long, hard name by the time he reached the fruit tree.

At last, the monkey thought of a trick. Perhaps you do not know it, but the monkey can play the guitar. He always played when the beasts gathered together in the garden to dance. The monkey went to the tiny house of the little old woman, carrying his guitar under his arm.

When she told him the long hard name of the wonderful fruit tree he made up a little tune to it, all his own, and sang it over and over again all the way from the tiny house of the little old woman to the corner of the garden where the wonderful fruit tree grew. When any of the other beasts met him and asked him what new song he was singing to his guitar, he said never a word. He marched straight on, playing his little tune over and over again on his guitar and singing softly the long hard name.

At last he reached the corner of the garden where the wonderful fruit tree grew. He had never seen it look so beautiful. The rosy-cheeked fruit glowed in the bright sunlight. The monkey could hardly wait to make his bow, say the long hard name over twice and ask for the fruit with a 'please.'

What a beautiful colour and what a delicious odour that fruit had! The monkey had never in all his life been so near to anything which smelled so good. He took a big bite. What a face he made! That beautiful sweet smelling fruit was bitter and sour, and it had a nasty taste. He threw it away from him as far as he could.

The monkey never forgot the tree's long hard name and the little tune he had sung. Nor did he forget how the fruit tasted. He never took a bite of it again; but, after that, his favourite trick was to treat the other beasts to the wonderful fruit just to see them make faces when they tasted it.

From: Fairy Tales from Brazil

The Fall of the Spider Man

In OLDEN TIMES, the Spider Man lived in the sky-country.

He dwelt in a bright little house all by himself, where he weaved webs and long flimsy ladders by which people went back and forth from the sky to the earth. The Star-people often went at night to earth, where they roamed about as fairies of light, doing good deeds for women and little children, and they always went back and forth on the ladder of the Spider Man. The Spider Man had to work very hard, weaving his webs and spinning the yarn from which his ladders were made.

One day, when he had a short breathing-time from his toil, he looked down at the earth-country and there he saw many of the earth-people playing at games, or taking sweet sap from the maple trees, or gathering berries on the rolling hills; but most of the men were lazily idling and doing nothing. The women were all working, after the fashion of Native Americans in those days; the men were working but little.

And Spider Man said to himself, 'I should like to go to the earth-country where men idle their time away. I would marry four wives who would work for me while I would take life easy, for I need a rest.'

He was very tired of his work, for he was kept at it day and night, always spinning and weaving his webs. But when he asked for a rest, he was not allowed to stop; he was only kicked for his pains and called Sleepy Head, and Lazy-bones and other harsh names, and told to work harder.

Then he grew angry and he resolved to punish the Star-people because they kept him so hard at work. He thought that if he punished them and made himself a nuisance, they would be glad to be rid of him. So he hit upon a crafty plan.

Each night, when a Star-fairy was climbing back to the sky-country, just as he came near the top of the ladder, the Spider Man would cut the strands and the fairy would fall to earth with a great crash.

Night after night he did this, and he chuckled to himself as he saw the sky-fairies sprawling through the air and kicking their heels, while the earth-people looked up wonderingly at them and called them Shooting Stars.

Many Star-people fell to earth in this way because of the Spider Man's tricks, and they could never get back to the sky-country because of their broken limbs or their disfigured faces, for in the sky-country, the people all must have beautiful faces and forms.

But Spider Man's tricks brought him no good; the people would not drive him away because they needed his webs, and he was kept always at his tasks. At last, he decided to run away of his own accord, and one night when the Moon and the Stars had gone to work and the sun was asleep, he said farewell to the sky-country and let himself down to earth by one of his own strands of yarn, spinning it as he dropped down.

In the earth-country, he married four wives as he had planned, for he wanted them to work for him while he took his ease. He thought he had worked long enough. All went well for a time and the Spider Man was quite happy living his lazy and contented life.

Not a strand did he spin, nor a web did he weave.

No men on earth were working; only the women toiled. At last, Glooskap, who ruled upon the earth in that time, became very angry because the men in these parts were so lazy, and he sent Famine into their country to punish them for their sins. Famine came very stealthily into the land and gathered up all the corn and carried it off; then he called to him all the animals, and the birds, and the fish of the sea and river, and he took them away with him.

In all the land, there was nothing left to eat. Only water remained. The people were very hungry and they lived on water for many days. Sometimes they drank the water cold, sometimes hot, sometimes lukewarm, but at best it was but poor fare.

The Spider Man soon grew tired of this strange diet, for it did not satisfy his hunger to live always on water. It filled his belly and swelled him to a great size, but it brought him little nourishment or strength.

So he said, 'There must be good food somewhere in the world; I will go in search of it.'

That night, when all the world was asleep, he took a large bag and crept softly away from his four wives and set out on his quest for food. He did not want anyone to know where he was going. For several days, he travelled, living only on water; but he found no food, and the bag was still empty on his back. At last one day, he saw birds in the trees and he knew that he was near the border of the Hunger-Land.

That night in the forest, when he stopped at a stream to drink, he saw a tiny gleam of light far ahead of him through the trees. He hurried towards the light and soon he came upon a man with a great hump on his shoulders and scars on his face, and a light hanging at his back, with a shade on it which he could close and open at his will.

The Spider Man said, 'I am looking for food; tell me where I can find it.'

And the humped man with the light said, 'Do you want it for your people?'

But the Spider Man said, 'No, I want it for myself.'

Then the humped man laughed and said, 'You are near to the border of the Land of Plenty; follow me and I will give you food.'

Then he flashed the light at his back, opening and closing the shade so that the light flickered, and he set off quickly through the trees.

The Spider Man followed the light flashing in the darkness, but he had to go so fast that he was almost out of breath when he reached the house where the humped man had stopped. But the humped man only laughed when he saw the Spider Man coming puffing wearily along with his fat and swollen belly. He gave him a good fat meal and the Spider Man soon felt better after his long fast.

Then the humped man said, 'You are the Spider Man who once weaved webs in the sky. I, too, once dwelt in the star-country, and one dark night as I was climbing back from the earth-country on your ladder, carrying my lamp on my back to light the way, when I was near the sky you cut the strands of the web and I fell to the earth with a great crash. That is why I have a great hump on my back and scars on my face, and because of this I have never been allowed to go back to the sky-country of the stars.

'I roam the earth at nights as a forest fairy just as I did in the olden days, for I have my former power still with me, and I still carry my lamp at my back; it is the starlight from the sky-country. I shall never get back to the star-country while I have life. But some day when my work on earth is done, I shall go back. But although you were cruel to me I will give you food.'

The Spider Man remembered the nights he had cut the ladder strands, and he laughed to himself at the memory of the star-fairies falling to earth with a great crash. But the man with the light knew that now he had his chance to take vengeance on the Spider Man. The latter did not suspect evil. He was glad to get food at last.

Then the humped man said, 'I will give you four pots. You must not open them until you get home. They will then be filled with food, and thereafter always when you open them they will be packed with good food. And the food will never grow less.'

The Spider Man put the four pots in his bag and, slinging it over his shoulder, he set out for his home, well pleased with his success. After he had gone away, the humped man used his power to make him hungry. Yet for several days he travelled without opening the pots, for although he was almost starving, he wished to do as the humped man had told him. At last, he could wait no longer. He stopped near his home, took the pots out of the bag and opened them. They were filled with good food as he had been promised. In one was a fine meat stew; in another were many cooked vegetables; in another was bread made from Indian corn; and in another was luscious ripe fruit. He ate until he was full.

'He covered the pots, put them back in the bag, and hid the bag among the trees. Then, he went home. He had meanwhile taken pity on his people and he decided to invite the Chief and all the tribe to a feast the next evening, for the pots would be full, and the food would never decrease, and there would be enough for all. He thought the people would regard him as a very wonderful man if he could supply them all with good food in their hunger.

When he reached his home, his wives were very glad to see him back, and they at once brought him water, the only food they had. But he laughed them to scorn, and threw the water in their faces and said, 'Oh, foolish women, I do not want water; it is not food for a great man like me. I have had a good meal of meat stew and corn bread and cooked vegetables and luscious ripe fruit. I know where much food is to be found, but I alone know. I can find food when all others fail, for I am a great man. Go forth and invite the Chief and all the people to a feast which I shall provide for them tomorrow night – a feast for all the land, for my food never grows less.'

They were all amazed when they heard his story, and the thought of his good meal greatly added to their hunger. But they went out and summoned all the tribe to a feast as he had told them.

The next night, all the people gathered for the feast, for the news of it had spread through all the land. They had taken no water that day, for they wished to eat well, and they were very hungry. They were as hungry as wild beasts in search of food. The Spider Man was very glad because the people praised him, and he proudly brought in his bag of pots. The people all waited hungrily and eagerly. But when he uncovered the first pot, there was no food there; he uncovered the second pot, but there was no food there; he uncovered all the pots, but not a bit of food was in any of them. They were all empty, and in the bottom of each was a great gaping hole.

Now it had happened in this way. When the humped man, the Star-fairy, had given the pots to the Spider Man, he knew well that the Spider Man would disobey his orders and that he would open the pots before he reached his home. He chuckled to himself, for he knew that now he could take vengeance on the web-weaver who had injured him.

So, when the Spider Man had left the pots among the trees, the humped man used his magic power and made holes in the pots, and the charm of the food was broken and all the food disappeared. When the people saw the empty pots, they thought they had been purposely deceived.

The remains of the food and the smell of stew and of fruit still clung to the pots. They thought the Spider Man had eaten all the food himself. So in their great hunger and their rage and their disappointment, they fell upon him and beat him and bore him to the ground, while the humped man with the lamp at his back hiding behind the trees looked on and laughed in his glee.

Then the people split the Spider Man's arms to the shoulders, and his legs to the thighs, so that he had eight limbs instead of four. And the humped man – the star-fairy named Firefly – came forth from behind the trees and standing over the fallen Spider Man he said, 'Henceforth, because of your cruelty to the star-people, you will always crawl on eight legs, and you will have a fat round belly because of the water you have drunk; and sometimes you will live on top of the water. But you shall always eat only flies and insects.

'And you will always spin downwards but never upwards, and you will often try to get back to the star-country, but you shall always slip down again on the strand of yarn you have spun.'

Then firefly flashed his light and went quickly away, opening and closing the shade of his lamp as he flitted among the trees.

And to this day, the Spider Man lives as the humped man of the lamp had spoken, because of the cruelty he practised on the star-fairies in the olden days.

From: Canadian Fairy Tales

Why the Bat is Ashamed to be Seen in the Daytime

THERE WAS ONCE an old mother sheep who had seven lambs, and one day the bat, who was about to make a visit to his father-in-law who lived a long day's march away, went to the old sheep and asked her to lend him one of her young lambs to carry his load for him.

At first, the mother sheep refused, but as the young lamb was anxious to travel and see something of the world, and begged to be allowed to go, at last she reluctantly consented. So, in the morning at daylight, the bat and the lamb set off together, the lamb carrying the bat's drinking-horn.

When they reached halfway, the bat told the lamb to leave the horn underneath a bamboo tree. Directly he arrived at the house, he sent the lamb back to get the horn. When the lamb had gone, the bat's father-in-law brought him food, and the bat ate it all, leaving nothing for the lamb. When the lamb returned, the bat said to him, 'Hello! you have arrived at last I see, but you are too late for food; it is all finished.'

He then sent the lamb back to the tree with the horn, and when the lamb returned again, it was late, and he went supperless to bed.

The next day, just before it was time for food, the bat sent the lamb off again for the drinking-horn, and when the food arrived, the bat, who was very greedy, ate it all up a second time. This mean behaviour on the part of the bat went on for four days, until at last, the lamb became quite thin and weak. The bat decided to return home the next day, and it was all the lamb could do to carry his load.

When he got home to his mother, the lamb complained bitterly of the treatment he had received from the bat, and was baa-ing all night, complaining of pains in his inside. The old mother sheep, who was very fond of her children, determined to be revenged on the bat for the cruel way he had starved her lamb; she therefore decided to consult the tortoise, who, although very poor, was considered by all people to be the wisest of all animals.

When the old sheep had told the whole story to the tortoise, he considered for some time, and then told the sheep that she might leave the matter entirely to him, and he would take ample revenge on the bat for his cruel treatment of her son.

Very soon after this, the bat thought he would again go and see his father-in-law, so he went to the mother sheep again and asked her for one of her sons to carry his load as before. The tortoise, who happened to be present, told the bat that he was going in that direction, and would cheerfully carry his load for him.

They set out on their journey the following day, and when they arrived at the halfway halting-place, the bat pursued the same tactics that he had on the previous occasion. He told the tortoise to hide his drinking-horn under the same tree as the lamb had hidden it before; this the tortoise did, but when the bat was not looking, he picked up the drinking-horn again and hid it in his bag.

When they arrived at the house, the tortoise hung the horn up out of sight in the back yard, and then sat down in the house. Just before it was time for food, the bat sent the tortoise to get the drinking-horn, and the tortoise went outside into the yard, and waited until he heard that the beating of the boiled yams into foo-foo had finished; he then went into the house and gave the drinking-horn to the bat, who was so surprised and angry, that when the food was passed, he refused to eat any of it, so the tortoise ate it all; this went on for four days, until at last, the bat became as thin as the poor little lamb had been on the previous occasion. At last, the bat could stand the pains of his inside no longer, and secretly told his mother-in-law to bring him food when the tortoise was not looking.

He said, 'I am now going to sleep for a little, but you can wake me up when the food is ready.'

The tortoise, who had been listening all the time, being hidden in a corner out of sight, waited until the bat was fast asleep, and then carried him very gently into the next room and placed him on his own bed; he then very softly and quietly took off the bat's cloth and covered himself in it, and lay down where the bat had been; very soon, the bat's mother-in-law brought the food and placed it next to where the bat was supposed to be sleeping, and having pulled his cloth to wake him, went away.

The tortoise then got up and ate all the food; when he had finished, he carried the bat back again, and took some of the palm oil and foo-foo and placed it inside the bat's lips while he was asleep; then the tortoise went to sleep himself.

In the morning when he woke up, the bat was hungrier than ever, and in a very bad temper, so he sought out his mother-in-law and started scolding her and asked her why she had not brought his food as he had told her to do.

She replied she had brought his food, and that he had eaten it; but this the bat denied and accused the tortoise of having eaten the food. The woman then said she would call the people in, and they should decide the matter; but the tortoise slipped out first and told the people that the best way to find out who had eaten the food was to make both the bat and himself rinse their mouths out with clean water into a basin.

This they decided to do, so the tortoise got his tooth-stick which he always used, and having cleaned his teeth properly, washed his mouth out, and returned to the house.

When all the people had arrived, the woman told them how the bat had abused her, and as he still maintained stoutly that he had had no food for five days, the people said that both he and the tortoise should wash their mouths out with clean water into two clean calabashes; this was done, and at once it could clearly be seen that the bat had been eating, as there were distinct traces of the palm-oil and foo-foo which the tortoise had put inside his lips floating on the water.

When the people saw this, they decided against the bat, and he was so ashamed that he ran away then and there and has ever since always hidden himself in the bush during the daytime, so that no one could see him, and only comes out at night to get his food.

The next day, the tortoise returned to the mother sheep and told her what he had done, and that the bat was forever disgraced. The old sheep praised him very much, and told all her friends, in consequence of which the reputation of the tortoise for wisdom was greatly increased throughout the whole country.

From: Folk Stories from Southern Nigeria

Aponibolinayen & the Sun

ONE DAY, APONIBOLINAYEN and her sister-in-law went out to gather greens.

They walked to the woods to the place where the siksiklat grew, for the tender leaves of this vine are very good to eat. Suddenly while searching about in the underbrush, Aponibolinayen cried out with joy, for she had found the vine, and she started to pick the leaves.

Pull as hard as she would, however, the leaves did not come loose, and all at once the vine wound itself around her body and began carrying her upward.

Far up through the air she went, until she reached the sky, and there the vine set her down under a tree. Aponibolinayen was so surprised to find herself in the sky that for some time she just sat and looked around, and then, hearing a rooster crow, she arose to see if she could find it.

Not far from where she had sat was a beautiful spring surrounded by tall betel-nut trees whose tops were pure gold. Rare beads were the sands of the spring, and the place where the women set their jars when they came to dip water was a large golden plate.

As Aponibolinayen stood admiring the beauties of this spring, she beheld a small house nearby, and she was filled with fear lest the owner should find her there. She looked about for some means of escape, and finally climbed to the top of a betel-nut tree and hid.

Now the owner of this house was Ini-init, the sun, but he was never at home in the daylight, for it was his duty to shine in the sky and give light to all the world. At the close of the day, when the Big Star took his place in the sky to shine through the night, Ini-init returned to his house, but early the next morning, he was always off again.

From her place in the top of the betel-nut tree, Aponibolinayen saw the sun when he came home at evening time, and again the next morning she saw him leave. When she was sure that he was out of sight, she climbed down and entered his dwelling, for she was very hungry. She cooked rice, and into a pot of boiling water she dropped a stick which immediately became fish, so that she had all she wished to eat. When she was no longer hungry, she lay down on the bed to sleep.

Now late in the afternoon, Ini-init returned from his work and went to fish in the river near his house, and he caught a big fish. While he sat on the bank cleaning his catch, he happened to look up toward his house and was startled to see that it appeared to be on fire. He hurried home, but when he reached the house, he saw that it was not burning at all, and he entered.

On his bed he beheld what looked like a flame of fire, but upon going closer, he found that it was a beautiful woman fast asleep.

Ini-init stood for some time wondering what he should do, and then he decided to cook some food and invite this lovely creature to eat with him. He put rice over the fire to boil and cut into pieces the fish he had caught.

The noise of this awakened Aponibolinayen, and she slipped out of the house and back to the top of the betel-nut tree. The sun did not see her leave, and when the food was prepared, he called her, but the bed was empty and he had to eat alone.

That night, Ini-init could not sleep well, for all the time he wondered who the beautiful woman could be. The next morning, however, he rose as usual and set forth to shine in the sky, for that was his work.

That day, Aponibolinayen stole again to the house of the sun and cooked food, and when she returned to the betel-nut tree, she left rice and fish ready for the sun when he came home.

Late in the afternoon Ini-init went into his home, and when he found pots of hot rice and fish over the fire, he was greatly troubled. After he had eaten, he walked a long time in the fresh air.

'Perhaps it is done by the lovely woman who looks like a flame of fire,' he said. 'If she comes again, I will try to catch her.'

The next day, the sun shone in the sky as before, and when the afternoon grew late, he called to the Big Star to hurry to take his place, for he was impatient to reach home. As he drew near the house, he saw that it again looked as if it was on fire. He crept quietly up the ladder, and when he had reached the top, he sprang in and shut the door behind him.

Aponibolinayen, who was cooking rice over the fire, was surprised and angry that she had been caught; but the sun gave her betel-nut which was covered with gold, and they chewed together and told each other their names. Then Aponibolinayen took up the rice and fish, and as they ate, they talked together and became acquainted.

After some time, Aponibolinayen and the sun were married, and every morning the sun went to shine in the sky, and upon his return at night he found his supper ready for him. He began to be troubled, however, to know where the food came from, for though he brought home a fine fish every night, Aponibolinayen always refused to cook it.

One night, he watched her prepare their meal, and he saw that, instead of using the nice fish he had brought, she only dropped a stick into the pot of boiling water.

'Why do you try to cook a stick?' asked Ini-init in surprise.

'So that we can have fish to eat,' answered his wife.

'If you cook that stick for a month, it will not be soft,' said Ini-init. 'Take this fish that I caught in the net, for it will be good.'

But Aponibolinayen only laughed at him, and when they were ready to eat, she took the cover off the pot and there was plenty of nice soft fish. The next night and the next, Aponibolinayen cooked the stick, and Ini-init became greatly troubled, for he saw that, though the stick always supplied them with fish, it never grew smaller.

Finally, he asked Aponibolinayen again why it was that she cooked the stick instead of the fish he brought, and she said: 'Do you not know of the woman on earth who has magical power and can change things?'

'Yes,' answered the sun, 'and now I know that you have great power.'

'Well, then,' said his wife, 'do not ask again why I cook the stick.'

And they ate their supper of rice and the fish which the stick made.

One night not long after this, Aponibolinayen told her husband that she wanted to go with him the next day when he made light in the sky.

'Oh, no, you cannot,' said the sun, 'for it is very hot up there, and you cannot stand the heat.'

'We will take many blankets and pillows,' said the woman, 'and when the heat becomes very great, I will hide under them.'

Again and again, Ini-init begged her not to go, but as often she insisted on accompanying him, and early in the morning they set out, carrying with them many blankets and pillows.

First, they went to the East, and as soon as they arrived, the sun began to shine, and Aponibolinayen was with him. They travelled toward the West, but when morning had passed into noontime, and they had reached the middle of the sky, Aponibolinayen was so hot that she melted and became oil. Then Ini-init put her into a bottle and wrapped her in the blankets and pillows and dropped her down to earth.

Now, one of the women of Aponibolinayen's town was at the spring dipping water when she heard something fall near her. Turning to look, she beheld a bundle of beautiful blankets and pillows which she began to unroll, and inside she found the most beautiful woman she had ever seen. Frightened at her discovery, the woman ran as fast as she could to the town, where she called the people together and told them to come at once to the spring. They all hastened to the spot, and there they found Aponibolinayen for whom they had been searching everywhere.

'Where have you been?' asked her father; 'we have searched all over the world and we could not find you.'

'I have come from Pindayan,' answered Aponibolinayen. 'Enemies of our people kept me there till I made my escape while they were asleep at night.'

All were filled with joy that the lost one had returned, and they decided that at the next moon, they would perform a ceremony for the spirits and invite all the relatives who were mourning for Aponibolinayen.

So, they began to prepare for the ceremony, and while they were pounding rice, Aponibolinayen asked her mother to prick her little finger where it itched, and as she did so a beautiful baby boy popped out. The people were very much surprised at this, and they noticed that every time he was bathed, the baby grew very fast so that, in a short time, he was able to walk. Then they were anxious to know who was the husband of Aponibolinayen, but she would not tell them, and they decided to invite everyone in the world to the ceremony that they might not overlook him.

They sent for the betel-nuts that were covered with gold, and when they had oiled them they commanded them to go to all the towns and compel the people to come to the ceremony.

'If anyone refuses to come, grow on his knee,' said the people, and the betel-nuts departed to do as they were bidden.

As the guests began to arrive, the people watched carefully for one who might be the husband of Aponibolinayen, but none appeared and they were greatly troubled. Finally, they went to the old woman, Alokotan, who was able to talk with the spirits, and begged her to find what town had not been visited by the betel-nuts which had been sent to invite the people. After she had consulted the spirits the old woman said:

'You have invited all the people except Ini-init who lives up above. Now you must send a betel-nut to summon him. It may be that he is the husband of Aponibolinayen, for the siksiklat vine carried her up when she went to gather greens.'

So a betel-nut was called and bidden to summon Ini-init.

The betel-nut went up to the sun, who was in his house, and said:

'Good morning, sun. I have come to summon you to a ceremony which the father and mother of Aponibolinayen are making for the spirits. If you do not want to go, I will grow on your head.'

'Grow on my head,' said the sun.

'I do not wish to go.'

So the betel-nut jumped upon his head and grew until it became so tall that the sun was not able to carry it, and he was in great pain.

'Oh, grow on my pig,' begged the sun. So the betel-nut jumped upon the pig's head and grew, but it was so heavy that the pig could not carry it and squealed all the time. At last the sun saw that he would have to obey the summons, and he said to the betel-nut:

'Get off my pig and I will go.'

So Ini-init came to the ceremony, and as soon as Aponibolinayen and the baby saw him, they were very happy and ran to meet him. Then the people knew that this was the husband of Aponibolinayen, and they waited eagerly for him to come up to them. As he drew near, however, they saw that he did not walk, for he was round; and then they perceived that he was not a man but a large stone.

All her relatives were very angry to find that Aponibolinayen had married a stone; and they compelled her to take off her beads and her good clothes, for, they said, she must now dress in old clothes and go again to live with the stone.

So Aponibolinayen put on the rags that they brought her and at once set out with the stone for his home. No sooner had they arrived there, however, than he became a handsome man, and they were very happy.

'In one moon,' said the sun, 'we will make a ceremony for the spirits, and I will pay your father and mother the marriage price for you.'

This pleased Aponibolinayen very much, and they used magic so that they had many neighbours who came to pound rice for them and to build a large spirit house.

Then they sent oiled betel-nuts to summon their relatives to the ceremony. The father of Aponibolinayen did not want to go, but the betel-nut threatened to grow on his knee if he did not. So he commanded all the people in the town to wash their hair and their clothes, and when all was ready they set out.

When they reached the town they were greatly surprised to find that the stone had become a man, and they chewed the magic betel-nuts to see who he might be. It was discovered that he was the son of a couple in Aponibolinayen's own town, and the people all rejoiced that this couple had found the son whom they had thought lost. They named him Aponitolau, and his parents paid the marriage price for his wife – the spirit house nine times full of valuable jars.

After that all danced and made merry for one moon, and when the people departed for their homes Ini-init and his wife went with them to live on the earth.

From: Philippine Folk Tales

The Tale of the Silver Saucer
& the Transparent Apple

THERE WAS ONCE an old peasant, and he must have had more brains under his hair than ever I had, for he was a merchant, and used to take things every year to sell at the big fair of Nijni Novgorod. Well, I could never do that. I could never be anything better than an old forester.

'Never mind, grandfather,' said Maroosia.

God knows best, and He makes some merchants and some foresters, and some good and some bad, all in His own way. Anyhow this one was a merchant, and he had three daughters. They were none of them so bad to look at, but one of them was as pretty as Maroosia.

And she was the best of them too.

The others put all the hard work on her, while they did nothing but look at themselves in the looking-glass and complain of what they had to eat. They called the pretty one 'Little Stupid,' because she was so good and did all their work for them. Oh, they were real bad ones, those two. We wouldn't have them in here for a minute.

Well, the time came round for the merchant to pack up and go to the big fair. He called his daughters, and said, 'Little pigeons,' just as I say to you.

'Little pigeons,' says he, 'what would you like me to bring you from the fair?'

Says the eldest, 'I'd like a necklace, but it must be a rich one.'

Says the second, 'I want a new dress with gold hems.'

But the youngest, the good one, Little Stupid, said nothing at all.

'Now little one,' says her father, 'what is it you want? I must bring something for you too.'

Says the little one, 'Could I have a silver saucer and a transparent apple? But never mind if there are none.'

The old merchant says, 'Long hair, short sense,' just as I say to Maroosia; but he promised the little pretty one, who was so good that her sisters called her stupid, that if he could get her a silver saucer and a transparent apple she should have them.

Then they all kissed each other, and he cracked his whip, and off he went, with the little bells jingling on the horses' harness.

The three sisters waited till he came back. The two elder ones looked in the looking glass and thought how fine they would look in the new necklace and the new dress; but the little pretty one took care of her old mother, and scrubbed and dusted and swept and cooked, and every day the other two said that the soup was burnt or the bread not properly baked.

Then one day there were a jingling of bells and a clattering of horses' hooves, and the old merchant came driving back from the fair.

The sisters ran out.

'Where is the necklace?' asked the first.

'You haven't forgotten the dress?' asked the second.

But the little one, Little Stupid, helped her old father off with his coat, and asked him if he was tired.

'Well, little one,' says the old merchant, 'and don't you want your fairing too? I went from one end of the market to the other before I could get what you wanted. I bought the silver saucer from an old merchant, and the transparent apple from a Finnish hag.'

'Oh, thank you, father,' says the little one.

'And what will you do with them?' says he.

'I shall spin the apple in the saucer,' says the little pretty one, and at that the old merchant burst out laughing. 'They don't call you 'Little Stupid' for nothing,' says he.

Well, they all had their fairings, and the two elder sisters, the bad ones, ran off and put on the new dress and the new necklace, and came out and strutted about, preening themselves like herons, now on one leg and now on the other, to see how they looked.

But Little Stupid, she just sat herself down beside the stove, and took the transparent apple and set it in the silver saucer, and she laughed softly to herself. And then she began spinning the apple in the saucer.

Round and round the apple spun in the saucer, faster and faster, till you couldn't see the apple at all, nothing but a mist like a little whirlpool in the silver saucer. And the little good one looked at it, and her eyes shone like yours.

Her sisters laughed at her.

'Spinning an apple in a saucer and staring at it, the little stupid,' they said, as they strutted about the room, listening to the rustle of the new dress and fingering the bright round stones of the necklace.

But the little pretty one did not mind them. She sat in the corner watching the spinning apple. And as it spun, she talked to it. 'Spin, spin, apple in the silver saucer.' This is what she said. 'Spin so that I may see the world. Let me have a peep at the little father tzar on his high throne. Let me see the rivers and the ships and the great towns far away.'

And as she looked at the little glass whirlpool in the saucer, there was the tzar, the little father – God preserve him! – sitting on his high throne. Ships sailed on the seas, their white sails swelling in the wind. There was Moscow with its white stone walls and painted churches. Why, there were the market at Nijni Novgorod, and the Arab merchants with their camels, and the Chinese with their blue trousers and bamboo staves. And then there was the great river Volga, with men on the banks towing ships against the stream. Yes, and she saw a sturgeon asleep in a deep pool.

'Oh! Oh! Oh!' said the little pretty one, as she saw all these things.

And the bad ones, they saw how her eyes shone, and they came and looked over her shoulder, and saw how all the world was there, in the spinning apple and the silver saucer.

And the old father came and looked over her shoulder too, and he saw the market at Nijni Novgorod.

'Why, there is the inn where I put up the horses,' said he. 'You haven't done so badly after all, Little Stupid.'

And the little pretty one, Little Stupid, went on staring into the glass whirlpool in the saucer, spinning the apple, and seeing all the world she had never seen before, floating there before her in the saucer, brighter than leaves in sunlight.

The bad ones, the elder sisters, were sick with envy.

'Little Stupid,' said the first, 'if you will give me your silver saucer and your transparent apple, I will give you my fine new necklace.'

'Little Stupid,' said the second, 'I will give you my new dress with gold hems if you will give me your transparent apple and your silver saucer.'

'Oh, I couldn't do that,' said the Little Stupid, and she went on spinning the apple in the saucer and seeing what was happening all over the world.

So, the bad ones put their wicked heads together and thought of a plan. And they took their father's axe and went into the deep forest and hid it under a bush.

The next day they waited till afternoon, when work was done, and the little pretty one was spinning her apple in the saucer.

Then they said, 'Come along, Little Stupid; we are all going to gather berries in the forest.'

'Do you really want me to come too?' says the little one. She would rather have played with her apple and saucer.

But they said, 'Why, of course. You don't think we can carry all the berries ourselves!'

So, the little one jumped up, and found the baskets, and went with them to the forest. But before she started, she ran to her father, who was counting his money, and was not too pleased to be interrupted, for figures go quickly out of your head when you have a lot of them to remember. She asked him to take care of the silver saucer and the transparent apple, for fear she would lose them in the forest.

'Very well, little bird,' says the old man, and he put the things in a box with a lock and key to it. He was a merchant, you know, and that sort are always careful about things, and go clattering about with a lot of keys at their belt. I've nothing to lock up, and never had, and perhaps it is just as well, for I could never be bothered with keys.

So, the little one picks up all three baskets and runs off after the others, the bad ones, with black hearts under their necklaces and new dresses.

They went deep into the forest, picking berries, and the little one picked so fast that she soon had a basket full. She was picking and picking and did not see what the bad ones were doing. They were fetching the axe.

The little one stood up to straighten her back, which ached after so much stooping, and she saw her two sisters standing in front of her, looking at her cruelly. Their baskets lay on the ground quite empty. They had not picked a berry. The eldest had the axe in her hand.

The little one was frightened.

'What is it, sisters?' says she; 'and why do you look at me with cruel eyes? And what is the axe for? You are not going to cut berries with an axe.'

'No, Little Stupid,' says the first, 'we are not going to cut berries with the axe.'

'No, Little Stupid,' says the second; 'the axe is here for something else.'

The little one begged them not to frighten her.

Says the first, 'Give me your transparent apple.'

Says the second, 'Give me your silver saucer.'

'If you don't give them up at once, we shall kill you.'

That is what the bad ones said.

The poor little one begged them. 'O darling sisters, do not kill me! I haven't got the saucer or the apple with me at all.'

'What a lie!' say the bad ones. 'You never would leave it behind.'

And one caught her by the hair, and the other swung the axe, and between them they killed the little pretty one, who was called Little Stupid because she was so good.

Then they looked for the saucer and the apple and could not find them. But it was too late now. So, they made a hole in the ground, and buried the little one under a birch tree.

When the sun went down, the bad ones came home and they wailed with false voices, and rubbed their eyes to make the tears come. They made their eyes red and their noses too, and they did not look any prettier for that.

'What is the matter with you, little pigeons?' said the old merchant and his wife.

I would not say 'little pigeons' to such bad ones. Black-hearted crows is what I would call them.

And they wailed and lamented aloud, 'We are miserable for ever. Our poor little sister is lost. We looked for her everywhere. We heard the wolves howling. They must have eaten her.'

The old mother and father cried like rivers in springtime, because they loved the little pretty one, who was called Little Stupid because she was so good.

But before their tears were dry, the bad ones began to ask for the silver saucer and the transparent apple.

'No, no,' says the old man; 'I shall keep them for ever, in memory of my poor little daughter whom God has taken away.'

So, the bad ones did not gain by killing their little sister.

'That is one good thing,' said Vanya.

'But is that all, grandfather?' said Maroosia.

'Wait a bit, little pigeons. Too much haste set his shoes on fire. You listen, and you will hear what happened,' said old Peter. He took a pinch of snuff from a little wooden box, and then he went on with his tale.

Time did not stop with the death of the little girl. Winter came, and the snow with it. Everything was all white, just as it is now. And the wolves came to the doors of the huts, even into the villages, and no one stirred farther than he need. And then the snow melted, and the buds broke on the trees, and the birds began singing, and the sun shone warmer every dry. The old people had almost forgotten the little pretty one who lay dead in the forest. The bad ones had not forgotten, because now they had to do the work, and they did not like that at all.

And then one day, some lambs strayed away into the forest, and a young shepherd went after them to bring them safely back to their mothers. And as he wandered this way and that through the forest, following their light tracks, he came to a little birch tree, bright with new leaves, waving over a little mound of earth.

And there was a reed growing in the mound, and that, you know as well as I, is a strange thing, one reed all by itself under a birch tree in the forest. But it was no stranger than the flowers, for there were flowers round it, some red as the sun at dawn and others blue as the summer sky.

Well, the shepherd looks at the reed, and he looks at those flowers, and he thinks, 'I've never seen anything like that before. I'll make a whistle-pipe of that reed and keep it for a memory till I grow old.'

So, he did. He cut the reed, and sat himself down on the mound, and carved away at the reed with his knife, and got the pith out of it by pushing a twig through it, and beating it gently till the bark swelled, made holes in it, and there was his whistle-pipe. And then he put it to his lips to see what sort of music he could make on it. But that he never knew, for before his lips touched it the whistle-pipe began playing by itself and reciting in a girl's sweet voice.

This is what it sang: 'Play, play, whistle-pipe. Bring happiness to my dear father and to my little mother. I was killed – yes, my life was taken from me in the deep forest for the sake of a silver saucer, for the sake of a transparent apple.'

When he heard that, the shepherd went back quickly to the village to show it to the people. And all the way the whistle-pipe went on playing and reciting, singing its little song.

And everyone who heard it said, 'What a strange song! But who is it who was killed?'

'I know nothing about it,' says the shepherd, and he tells them about the mound and the reed and the flowers, and how he cut the reed and made the whistle-pipe, and how the whistle-pipe does its playing by itself.

And as he was going through the village, with all the people crowding about him, the old merchant, that one who was the father of the two bad ones and of the little pretty one, came along and listened with the rest. And when he heard the words about the silver saucer and the transparent apple, he snatched the whistle-pipe from the shepherd boy.

And still it sang: 'Play, play, whistle-pipe! Bring happiness to my dear father and to my little mother. I was killed – yes, my life was taken from me in the deep forest for the sake of a silver saucer, for the sake of a transparent apple.'

And the old merchant remembered the little good one, and his tears trickled over his cheeks and down his old beard. Old men love little pigeons, you know. And he said to the shepherd, 'Take me at once to the mound, where you say you cut the reed.'

The shepherd led the way, and the old man walked beside him, crying, while the whistle-pipe in his hand went on singing and reciting its little song over and over again.

They came to the mound under the birch tree, and there were the flowers, shining red and blue, and there in the middle of the mound was the Stump of the reed which the shepherd had cut.

The whistle-pipe sang on and on.

Well, there and then they dug up the mound, and there was the little girl lying under the dark earth as if she were asleep.

'O God of mine,' says the old merchant, 'this is my daughter, my little pretty one, whom we called Little Stupid.'

He began to weep loudly and wring his hands; but the whistle-pipe, playing and reciting, changed its song. This is what it sang: 'My sisters took me into the forest to look for the red berries. In the deep forest, they killed poor me for the sake of a silver saucer, for the sake of a transparent apple. Wake me, dear father, from a bitter dream, by fetching water from the well of the tzar.'

How the people scowled at the two sisters! They scowled; they cursed them for the bad ones they were. And the bad ones, the two sisters, wept, and fell on their knees, and confessed everything. They were taken, and their hands were tied, and they were shut up in prison.

'Do not kill them,' begged the old merchant, 'for then I should have no daughters at all, and when there are no fish in the river, we make do with crays. Besides, let me go to the tzar and beg water from his well. Perhaps my little daughter will wake up, as the whistle-pipe tells us.'

And the whistle-pipe sang again: 'Wake me, wake me, dear father, from a bitter dream, by fetching water from the well of the tzar. Till then, dear father, a blanket of black earth and the shade of the green birch tree.'

So, they covered the little girl with her blanket of earth, and the shepherd with his dogs watched the mound night and day. He begged for the whistle-pipe to keep him company, poor lad, and all the days and nights he thought of the sweet face of the little pretty one he had seen there under the birch tree.

The old merchant harnessed his horse, as if he were going to the town; and he drove off through the forest, along the roads, till he came to the palace of the tzar, the little father of all good Russians. And then he left his horse and cart and waited on the steps of the palace.

The tzar, the little father, with rings on his fingers and a gold crown on his head, came out on the steps in the morning sunshine; and as for the old merchant, he fell on his knees and kissed the feet of the tzar, and begged, 'O little father, tzar, give me leave to take water – just a little drop of water – from your holy well.'

'And what will you do with it?' says the tzar.

'I will wake my daughter from a bitter dream,' says the old merchant. 'She was murdered by her sisters – killed in the deep forest – for the sake of a silver saucer, for the sake of a transparent apple.'

'A silver saucer?' says the tzar – 'a transparent apple? Tell me about that.'

And the old merchant told the tzar everything, just as I have told it to you.

And the tzar, the little father, he gave the old merchant a glass of water from his holy well.

'But,' says he, 'when your daughter wakes, bring her to me, and her sisters with her, and also the silver saucer and the transparent apple.'

The old man kissed the ground before the tzar and took the glass of water and drove home with it, and I can tell you he was careful not to spill a drop. He carried it all the way in one hand as he drove.

He came to the forest and to the flowering mound under the little birch tree, and there was the shepherd watching with his dogs. The old merchant and the shepherd took away the blanket of black earth. Tenderly, tenderly the shepherd used his fingers, until the little girl, the pretty one, the good one, lay there as sweet as if she were not dead.

Then the merchant scattered the holy water from the glass over the little girl. And his daughterkin blushed as she lay there, and opened her eyes, and passed a hand across them, as if she were waking from a dream. And then she leapt up, crying and laughing, and clung about her old father's neck. And there they stood, the two of them, laughing and crying with joy. And the shepherd could not take his eyes from her, and in his eyes, too, there were tears.

But the old father did not forget what he had promised the tzar. He set the little pretty one, who had been so good that her wicked sisters had called her Stupid, to sit beside him on the cart. And he brought something from the house in a coffer of wood and kept it under his coat. And they brought out the two sisters, the bad ones, from their dark prison, and set them in the cart.

And the Little Stupid kissed them and cried over them, and wanted to loose their hands, but the old merchant would not let her. And they all drove together till they came to the palace of the tzar. The shepherd boy could not take his eyes from the little pretty one, and he ran all the way behind the cart.

Well, they came to the palace, and waited on the steps; and the tzar came out to take the morning air, and he saw the old merchant, and the two sisters with their hands tied, and the little pretty, one, as lovely as a spring day. And the tzar saw her and could not take his eyes from her.

He did not see the shepherd boy, who hid away among the crowd.

Says the great tzar to his soldiers, pointing to the bad sisters, 'These two are to be put to death at sunset. When the sun goes down their heads must come off, for they are not fit to see another day.'

Then he turns to the little pretty one, and he says: 'Little sweet pigeon, where is your silver saucer, and where is your transparent apple?'

The old merchant took the wooden box from under his coat, and opened it with a key at his belt, and gave it to the little one, and she took out the silver saucer and the transparent apple and gave them to the tzar.

'O lord tzar,' says she, 'O little father, spin the apple in the saucer, and you will see whatever you wish to see – your soldiers, your high hills, your forests, your plains, your rivers, and Everything in all Russia.'

And the tzar, the little father, spun the apple in the saucer till it seemed a little whirlpool of white mist, and there he saw glittering towns, and regiments of soldiers marching to war, and ships, and day and night, and the clear stars above the trees. He looked at these things and thought much of them.

Then the little good one threw herself on her knees before him, weeping. 'O little father, tzar,' she says, 'take my transparent apple and my silver saucer; only forgive my sisters. Do not kill them because of me. If their heads are cut off when the sun goes down, it would have been better for me to lie under the blanket of black earth in the shade of the birch tree in the forest.'

The tzar was pleased with the kind heart of the little pretty one, and he forgave the bad ones, and their hands were untied, and the little pretty one kissed them, and they kissed her again and said they were sorry.

The old merchant looked up at the sun and saw how the time was going. 'Well, well,' says he, 'it's time we were getting ready to go home.'

They all fell on their knees before the tzar and thanked him. But the tzar could not take his eyes from the little pretty one and would not let her go. 'Little sweet pigeon,' says he, 'will you be my tzaritza, and a kind mother to Holy Russia?'

And the little good one did not know what to say.

She blushed and answered, very rightly, 'As my father orders, and as my little mother wishes, so shall it be.'

The tzar was pleased with her answer, and he sent a messenger on a galloping horse to ask leave from the little pretty one's old mother. And of course, the old mother said that she was more than willing. So that was all right. Then there was a wedding – such a wedding! – and every city in Russia sent a silver plate of bread, and a golden salt-cellar, with their good wishes to the tzar and tzaritza.

Only the shepherd boy, when he heard that the little pretty one was to marry the tzar, turned sadly away and went off into the forest.

'Are you happy, little sweet pigeon?' says the tzar.

'Oh yes,' says the Little Stupid, who was now tzaritza and mother of Holy Russia; 'but there is one thing that would make me happier.'

'And what is that?' says the lord tzar.

'I cannot bear to lose my old father and my little mother and my dear sisters. Let them be with me here in the palace, as they were in my father's house.'

The tzar laughed at the little pretty one, but he agreed, and the little pretty one ran to tell them the good news. She said to her sisters, 'Let all be forgotten, and all be forgiven, and may the evil eye fall on the one who first speaks of what has been!'

For a long time, the tzar lived, and the little pretty one the tzaritza, and they had many children, and were very happy together. And ever since then the tzars of Russia have kept the silver saucer and the transparent apple, so that, whenever they wish, they can see everything that is going on all over Russia. Perhaps even now the tzar, the little father – God preserve him! – is spinning the apple in the saucer, and looking at us, and thinking it is time that two little pigeons were in bed.

'Is that the end?' said Vanya.

'That is the end,' said old Peter.

'Poor shepherd boy!' said Maroosia.

'I don't know about that,' said old Peter.

'You see, if he had married the little pretty one, and had to have all the family to live with him, he would have had them in a hut like ours instead of in a great palace, and so he would never have had room to get away from them. And now, little pigeons, who is going to be first into bed?'

From: Old Peter's Russian Tales

The Fairies of Caragonan

ONCE UPON A time, a great many fairies lived in Mona.

One day, the queen fairy's daughter, who was now fifteen years of age, told her mother she wished to go out and see the world.

The queen consented, allowing her to go for a day, and to change from a fairy to a bird, or from a bird to a fairy, as she wished.

When she returned one night she said: 'I've been to a gentleman's house, and as I stood listening, I heard the gentleman was witched: he was very ill, and crying out with pain.'

'Oh, I must look into that,' said the queen.

So, the next day she went through her process and found that he was bewitched by an old witch. So, the following day she set out with six other fairies, and when they came to the gentleman's house she found he was very ill.

Going into the room, bearing a small blue pot they had brought with them, the queen asked him: 'Would you like to be cured?'

'Oh, bless you; yes, indeed.'

Whereupon the queen put the little blue pot of perfume on the centre of the table, and lit it, when the room was instantly filled with the most delicious odour.

Whilst the perfume was burning, the six fairies formed in line behind her, and she leading, they walked round the table three times, chanting in chorus:

'Round and round three times three,
We have come to cure thee.'

At the end of the third round, she touched the burning perfume with her wand, and then touched the gentleman on the head, saying: 'Be thou made whole.'

No sooner had she said the words than he jumped up hale and hearty, and said: 'Oh, dear queen, what shall I do for you? I'll do anything you wish.'

'Money, I do not wish for,' said the queen, 'but there's a little plot of ground on the sea-cliff I want you to lend me, for I wish to make a ring there, and the grass will die when I make the ring. Then, I want you to build three walls around the ring, but leave the sea-side open, so that we may be able to come and go easily.'

'With the greatest of pleasure,' said the gentleman; and he built the three stone walls at once, at the spot indicated.

Near the gentleman lived the old witch, and she had the power of turning at will into a hare. The gentleman was a great hare hunter, but the hounds could never catch this hare; it always disappeared in a mill, running between the wings and jumping in at an open window, though they stationed two men and a dog at the spot, when it immediately turned into the old witch.

And the old miller never suspected, for the old woman used to take him a peck of corn to grind a few days before any hunt, telling him she would call for it on the afternoon of the day of the hunt. So that when she arrived, she was expected.

One day, she had been taunting the gentleman as he returned from a hunt, that he could never catch the hare, and he struck her with his whip, saying, 'Get away, you witchcraft!'

Whereupon she witched him, and he fell ill, and was cured as we have seen.

When he got well, he watched the old witch, and saw she often visited the house of an old miser who lived nearby with his beautiful niece. Now all the people in the village touched their hats most respectfully to this old miser, for they knew he had dealings with the witch, and they were as much afraid of him as of her; but everyone loved the miser's kind and beautiful niece.

When the fairies got home, the queen told her daughter: 'I have no power over the old witch for twelve months from today, and then I have no power over her life. She must lose that by the arm of a man.'

So, the next day the daughter was sent out again to see whether she could find a person suited to that purpose.

In the village lived a small crofter who was afraid of nothing; he was the boldest man thereabouts; and one day he passed the miser without saluting him. The old fellow went off at once and told the witch.

'Oh, I'll settle his cows tonight!' said she, and they were taken sick, and gave no milk that night.

The fairy's daughter arrived at his croft-yard after the cows were taken ill, and she heard him say to his son, a bright lad: 'It must be the old witch!'

When she heard this, she sent him to the queen.

So next day, the fairy queen took six fairies and went to the croft, taking her blue pot of perfume. When she got there, she asked the crofter if he would like his cows cured?

'God bless you, yes!' he said.

The queen made him bring a round table into the yard, whereon she placed the blue pot of perfume, and having lit it, as before, they formed in line and walked round thrice, chanting the words:

'Round and round three times three,
We have come to cure thee.'

Then, she dipped the end of her wand into the perfume, and touched the cows on the forehead, saying to each one: 'Be thou whole.' Whereupon they jumped up, cured.

The little farmer was overjoyed, and cried: 'Oh, what can I do for you? What can I do for you?'

'Money, I care not for,' said the queen, 'all I want is your son to avenge you and me.'

The lad jumped up and said: 'What I can do I'll do it for you, my lady fairy.'

She told him to be at the walled plot the following day at noon and left.

The next day at noon, the queen and her daughter and three hundred other fairies came up the cliff to the green grass plot, and they carried a pole, and a tape, and a mirror. When they reached the plot they planted the pole in the ground and hung the mirror on the pole.

The queen took the tape, which measured ten yards and was fastened to the top of the pole, and walked round in a circle, and wherever she set her feet the grass withered and died.

Then the fairies followed up behind the queen, and each fairy carried a harebell in her left hand, and a little blue cup of burning perfume in her right.

When they had formed up, the queen called the lad to her side and told him to walk by her throughout. They then started off, all singing in chorus:

'Round and round three times three,
Tell me what you see.'

When they finished the first round, the queen and lad stopped before the mirror, and she asked the lad what he saw?

'I see, I see, the mirror tells me,
It is the witch that I see,' said the lad.

So, they marched round again, singing the same words as before, and when they stopped a second time before the mirror the queen again asked him what he saw?

'I see, I see, the mirror tells me,
It is a hare that I see,' said the lad.

A third time the ceremony and question were repeated.

'I see, I see, the mirror tells me,
The hares run up the hill to the mill.'

'Now,' said the queen, 'there is to be a hare-hunting this day week; be at the mill at noon, and I will meet you there.'

And then the fairies, pole, mirror, and all, vanished and only the empty ring on the green was left.

Upon the appointed day, the lad went to his tryst, and at noon the fairy queen appeared, and gave him a sling, and a smooth pebble from the beach, saying:

'I have blessed your arms, and I have blessed the sling
    and the stone.
Now as the clock strikes three,
Go up the hill near the mill,
And in the ring stand still
Till you hear the click of the mill.
Then with thy arm, with power and might,
You shall strike and smite
The devil of a witch called Jezabel light,
And you shall see an awful sight.'

The lad did as he was bidden, and presently he heard the huntsman's horn and the hue and cry and saw the hare running down the opposite hillside, where the hounds seemed to gain on her, but as she breasted the hill on which he stood she gained on them.

As she came towards the mill he threw his stone, and it lodged in her skull, and when he ran up, he found he had killed the old witch.

As the huntsmen came up, they crowded round him, and praised him; and then they fastened the witch's body to a horse by ropes, and dragged her to the bottom of the valley, where they buried her in a ditch. That night, when the miser heard of her death, he dropped down dead on the spot.

As the lad was going home, the queen appeared to him and told him to be at the ring the following day at noon.

Next day, all the fairies came with the pole and mirror, each carrying a harebell in her left hand, and a blue cup of burning perfume in her right, and they formed up as before, the lad walking beside the queen. They marched round and repeated the old words, when the queen stopped before the mirror, and said:

'What do you see?'
'I see, I see, the mirror tells me,
It is an old plate – cupboard that I see.'

A second time they went round, and the question, was repeated.

'I see, I see, the mirror tells me,
'The back is turned to me.'

A third time was the ceremony fulfilled, and the lad answered,

'I see, I see, the mirror tells me,
'A spring-door is open to me.'

'Buy that plate-cupboard at the miser's sale,' said the queen, and she and her companions disappeared as before.

Upon the day of the sale, all the things were brought out in the road, and the cupboard was put up, the lad recognising it and bidding up for it till it was sold to him.

When he had paid for it, he took it home in a cart, and when he got in and examined it, he found the secret drawer behind was full of gold. The following week, the house and land, thirty acres, was put up for sale, and the lad bought both, and married the miser's niece, and they lived happily till they died.

From: Welsh Fairy Tales & Other Stories

Clever Manka: The Story of a Girl Who Knew What to Say

THERE WAS ONCE a rich farmer who was as grasping and unscrupulous as he was rich. He was always driving a hard bargain and always getting the better of his poor neighbours.

One of these neighbours was a humble shepherd who, in return for service, was to receive from the farmer a heifer. When the time of payment came, the farmer refused to give the shepherd the heifer and the shepherd was forced to lay the matter before the burgomaster.

The burgomaster, who was a young man and as yet not very experienced, listened to both sides, and when he had deliberated, he said: 'Instead of deciding this case, I will put a riddle to you both and the man who makes the best answer shall have the heifer. Are you agreed?'

The farmer and the shepherd accepted this proposal and the burgomaster said: 'Well then, here is my riddle: What is the swiftest thing in the world? What is the sweetest thing? What is the richest? Think out your answers and bring them to me at this same hour tomorrow.'

The farmer went home in a temper. 'What kind of a burgomaster is this young fellow!' he growled.

'If he had let me keep the heifer, I'd have sent him a bushel of pears. But now I'm in a fair way of losing the heifer for I can't think of any answer to his foolish riddle.'

'What is the matter, husband?' his wife asked.

'It's that new burgomaster. The old one would have given me the heifer without any argument, but this young man thinks to decide the case by asking us riddles.'

When he told his wife what the riddle was, she cheered him greatly by telling him that she knew the answers at once.

'Why, husband,' said she, 'our grey mare must be the swiftest thing in the world. You know yourself nothing ever passes us on the road. As for the sweetest, did you ever taste honey any sweeter than ours? And I'm sure there's nothing richer than our chest of golden ducats that we've been laying by these forty years.'

The farmer was delighted. 'You're right, wife, you're right! That heifer remains ours!'

The shepherd, when he got home, was downcast and sad. He had a daughter, a clever girl named Manka, who met him at the door of his cottage and asked: 'What is it, father? What did the burgomaster say?'

The shepherd sighed.

'I'm afraid I've lost the heifer. The burgomaster set us a riddle and I know I shall never guess it.'

'Perhaps I can help you,' Manka said. 'What is it?'

So, the shepherd gave her the riddle and the next day as he was setting out for the burgomaster's, Manka told him what answers to make.

When he reached the burgomaster's house, the farmer was already there rubbing his hands and beaming with self-importance.

The burgomaster again propounded the riddle and then asked the farmer his answers.

The farmer cleared his throat and with a pompous air began: 'The swiftest thing in the world? Why, my dear sir, that's my grey mare, of course, for no other horse ever passes us on the road. The sweetest? Honey from my beehives, to be sure. The richest? What can be richer than my chest of golden ducats!'

And the farmer squared his shoulders and smiled triumphantly.

'H'm,' said the young burgomaster, dryly. Then he asked: 'What answers does the shepherd make?'

The shepherd bowed politely and said: 'The swiftest thing in the world is thought, for thought can run any distance in the twinkling of an eye. The sweetest thing of all is sleep, for when a man is tired and sad what can be sweeter? The richest thing is the earth, for out of the earth come all the riches of the world.'

'Good!' the burgomaster cried. 'Good! The heifer goes to the shepherd!'

Later the burgomaster said to the shepherd: 'Tell me, now, who gave you those answers? I'm sure they never came out of your own head.'

At first the shepherd tried not to tell, but when the burgomaster pressed him, he confessed that they came from his daughter, Manka. The burgomaster, who thought he would like to make another test of Manka's cleverness, sent for ten eggs. He gave them to the shepherd and said: 'Take these eggs to Manka and tell her to have them hatched out by tomorrow and to bring me the chicks.'

When the shepherd reached home and gave Manka the burgomaster's message, Manka laughed and said: 'Take a handful of millet and go right back to the burgomaster. Say to him: "My daughter sends you this millet. She says that if you plant it, grow it, and have it harvested by tomorrow, she'll bring you the ten chicks and you can feed them the ripe grain."'

When the burgomaster heard this, he laughed heartily.

'That's a clever girl of yours,' he told the shepherd. 'If she's as comely as she is clever, I think I'd like to marry her. Tell her to come to see me, but she must come neither by day nor by night, neither riding nor walking, neither dressed nor undressed.'

When Manka received this message, she waited until the next dawn when night was gone and day not yet arrived. Then she wrapped herself in a fishnet and, throwing one leg over a goat's back and keeping one foot on the ground, she went to the burgomaster's house.

Now I ask you: did she go dressed? No, she wasn't dressed. A fishnet isn't clothing. Did she go undressed? Of course not, for wasn't she covered with a fishnet? Did she walk to the burgomaster's? No, she didn't walk, for she went with one leg thrown over a goat. Then did she ride? Of course, she didn't ride for wasn't she walking on one foot?

When she reached the burgomaster's house she called out: 'Here I am, Mr. Burgomaster, and I've come neither by day nor by night, neither riding nor walking, neither dressed nor undressed.'

The young burgomaster was so delighted with Manka's cleverness and so pleased with her comely looks that he proposed to her at once, and in a short time married her.

'But understand, my dear Manka,' he said, 'you are not to use that cleverness of yours at my expense. I won't have you interfering in any of my cases. In fact, if ever you give advice to anyone who comes to me for judgment, I'll turn you out of my house at once and send you home to your father.'

All went well for a time. Manka busied herself in her housekeeping and was careful not to interfere in any of the burgomaster's cases.

Then, one day, two farmers came to the burgomaster to have a dispute settled. One of the farmers owned a mare which had foaled in the marketplace. The colt had run under the wagon of the other farmer and thereupon the owner of the wagon claimed the colt as his property.

The burgomaster, who was thinking of something else while the case was being presented, said carelessly: 'The man who found the colt under his wagon is, of course, the owner of the colt.'

As the owner of the mare was leaving the burgomaster's house, he met Manka and stopped to tell her about the case. Manka was ashamed of her husband for making so foolish a decision and she said to the farmer: 'Come back this afternoon with a fishing net and stretch it across the dusty road. When the burgomaster sees you, he will come out and ask you what you are doing. Say to him that you're catching fish. When he asks you how you can expect to catch fish in a dusty road, tell him it's just as easy for you to catch fish in a dusty road as it is for a wagon to foal. Then he'll see the injustice of his decision and have the colt returned to you. But remember one thing: you mustn't let him find out that it was I who told you to do this.'

That afternoon when the burgomaster chanced to look out the window, he saw a man stretching a fishnet across the dusty road. He went out to him and asked: 'What are you doing?'

'Fishing.'

'Fishing in a dusty road? Are you daft?'

'Well,' the man said, 'it's just as easy for me to catch fish in a dusty road as it is for a wagon to foal.'

Then the burgomaster recognized the man as the owner of the mare, and he had to confess that what he said was true. 'Of course, the colt belongs to your mare and must be returned to you. But tell me,' he said, 'who put you up to this? You didn't think of it yourself.'

The farmer tried not to tell but the burgomaster questioned him until he found out that Manka was at the bottom of it. This made him very angry. He went into the house and called his wife.

'Manka,' he said, 'do you forget what I told you would happen if you went interfering in any of my cases? Home, you go this very day. I don't care to hear any excuses. The matter is settled. You may take with you the one thing you like best in my house for I won't have people saying that I treated you shabbily.'

Manka made no outcry.

'Very well, my dear husband, I shall do as you say: I shall go home to my father's cottage and take with me the one thing I like best in your house. But don't make me go until after supper. We have been very happy together and I should like to eat one last meal with you. Let us have no more words but be kind to each other as we've always been and then part as friends.'

The burgomaster agreed to this and Manka prepared a fine supper of all the dishes of which her husband was particularly fond. The burgomaster opened his choicest wine and pledged Manka's health.

Then he set to, and the supper was so good that he ate and ate and ate. And the more he ate, the more he drank until at last, he grew drowsy and fell sound asleep in his chair. Then without awakening him Manka had him carried out to the wagon that was waiting to take her home to her father.

The next morning when the burgomaster opened his eyes, he found himself lying in the shepherd's cottage.

'What does this mean?' he roared out.

'Nothing, dear husband, nothing!' Manka said. 'You know you told me I might take with me the one thing I liked best in your house, so of course I took you! That's all.'

For a moment the burgomaster rubbed his eyes in amazement. Then he laughed loud and heartily to think how Manka had outwitted him.

'Manka,' he said, 'you're too clever for me. Come on, my dear, let's go home.'

So, they climbed back into the wagon and drove home.

The burgomaster never again scolded his wife but thereafter whenever a very difficult case came up he always said: 'I think we had better consult my wife. You know, she's a very clever woman.'

From: The Shoemaker's Apron: A Second Book of
Czechoslovak Fairy Tales

The Little White Cat

A LONG, LONG time ago, in a valley far away, the giant Trencoss lived in a great castle, surrounded by trees that were always green. The castle had a hundred doors, and every door was guarded by a huge, shaggy hound, with tongue of fire and claws of iron, who tore to pieces anyone who went to the castle without the giant's leave.

Trencoss had made war on the king of the Torrents and, having killed the king, and slain his people, and burned his palace, he carried off his only daughter, the Princess Eileen, to the castle in the valley.

Here he provided her with beautiful rooms, and appointed a hundred dwarfs dressed in blue and yellow satin to wait upon her, and harpers to play sweet music for her, and he gave her diamonds without number, brighter than the sun; but he would not allow her to go outside the castle, and told her if she went one step beyond its doors, the hounds, with tongues of fire and claws of iron, would tear her to pieces.

A week after her arrival, war broke out between the giant and the king of the islands, and before he set out for battle, the giant sent for the princess, and informed her that on his return he would make her his wife. When the princess heard this, she began to cry, for she would rather die than marry the giant who had slain her father.

'Crying will only spoil your bright eyes, my little princess,' said Trencoss, 'and you will have to marry me whether you like it or no.'

He then bade her go back to her room, and he ordered the dwarfs to give her everything she asked for while he was away, and the harpers to play the sweetest music for her. When the princess gained her room, she cried as if her heart would break.

The long day passed slowly, and the night came, but brought no sleep to Eileen, and in the grey light of the morning she rose and opened the window, and looked about in every direction to see if there were any chance of escape.

But the window was ever so high above the ground, and below were the hungry and ever watchful hounds. With a heavy heart she was about to close the window when she thought she saw the branches of the tree that was nearest to it moving. She looked again, and she saw a little white cat creeping along one of the branches.

'Mew!' cried the cat.

'Poor little pussy,' said the princess. 'Come to me, pussy.'

'Stand back from the window,' said the cat, 'and I will.'

The princess stepped back, and the little white cat jumped into the room. The princess took the little cat on her lap and stroked him with her hand, and the cat raised up its back and began to purr.

'Where do you come from, and what is your name?' asked the princess.

'No matter where I come from or what's my name,' said the cat, 'I am a friend of yours, and I come to help you.'

'I never wanted help worse,' said the princess.

'I know that,' said the cat; 'and now listen to me. When the giant comes back from battle and asks you to marry him, say to him you will marry him.'

'But I will never marry him,' said the princess.

'Do what I tell you,' said the cat. 'When he asks you to marry him, say to him you will if his dwarfs will wind for you three balls from the fairy dew that lies on the bushes on a misty morning as big as these,' said the cat, putting his right forefoot into his ear and taking out three balls – one yellow, one red, and one blue.

'They are very small,' said the princess. 'They are not much bigger than peas, and the dwarfs will not be long at their work.'

'Won't they,' said the cat. 'It will take them a month and a day to make one, so that it will take three months and three days before the balls are wound; but the giant, like you, will think they can be made in a few days, and so he will readily promise to do what you ask. He will soon find out his mistake, but he will keep his word, and will not press you to marry him until the balls are wound.'

'When will the giant come back?' asked Eileen.

'He will return tomorrow afternoon,' said the cat.

'Will you stay with me until then?' said the princess. 'I am very lonely.'

'I cannot stay,' said the cat. 'I have to go away to my palace on the island on which no man ever placed his foot, and where no man but one shall ever come.'

'And where is that island?' asked the princess, 'and who is the man?'

'The island is in the far-off seas where vessel never sailed; the man you will see before many days are over; and if all goes well, he will one day slay the giant Trencoss and free you from his power.'

'Ah!' sighed the princess, 'that can never be, for no weapon can wound the hundred hounds that guard the castle, and no sword can kill the giant Trencoss.'

'There is a sword that will kill him,' said the cat; 'but I must go now. Remember what you are to say to the giant when he comes home, and every morning watch the tree on which you saw me, and if you see in the branches anyone you like better than yourself,' said the cat, winking at the princess, 'throw him these three balls and leave the rest to me; but take care not to speak a single word to him, for if you do, all will be lost.'

'Shall I ever see you again?' asked the princess.

'Time will tell,' answered the cat, and, without saying so much as goodbye, he jumped through the window on to the tree, and in a second was out of sight.

The morrow afternoon came, and the giant Trencoss returned from battle. Eileen knew of his coming by the furious barking of the hounds, and her heart sank, for she knew that in a few moments she would be summoned to his presence.

Indeed, he had hardly entered the castle when he sent for her and told her to get ready for the wedding.

The princess tried to look cheerful, as she answered: 'I will be ready as soon as you wish; but you must first promise me something.'

'Ask anything you like, little princess,' said Trencoss.

'Well, then,' said Eileen, 'before I marry you, you must make your dwarfs wind three balls as big as these from the fairy dew that lies on the bushes on a misty morning in summer.'

'Is that all?' said Trencoss, laughing. 'I shall give the dwarfs orders at once, and by this time tomorrow the balls will be wound, and our wedding can take place in the evening.'

'And will you leave me to myself until then?'

'I will,' said Trencoss.

'On your honour as a giant?' said Eileen.

'On my honour as a giant,' replied Trencoss.

The princess returned to her rooms, and the giant summoned all his dwarfs, and he ordered them to go forth in the dawning of the morn and to gather all the fairy dew lying on the bushes, and to wind three balls – one yellow, one red, and one blue.

The next morning, and the next, and the next, the dwarfs went out into the fields and searched all the hedgerows, but they could gather only as much fairy dew as would make a thread as long as a wee girl's eyelash; and so, they had to go out morning after morning, and the giant fumed and threatened, but all to no purpose.

He was very angry with the princess, and he was vexed with himself that she was so much cleverer than he was, and, moreover, he saw now that the wedding could not take place as soon as he expected.

When the little white cat went away from the castle, he ran as fast as he could up hill and down dale, and never stopped until he came to the prince of the Silver River. The prince was alone, and very sad and sorrowful he was, for he was thinking of the Princess Eileen, and wondering where she could be.

'Mew,' said the cat, as he sprang softly into the room; but the prince did not heed him. 'Mew,' again said the cat; but again, the prince did not heed him. 'Mew,' said the cat the third time, and he jumped up on the prince's knee.

'Where do you come from, and what do you want?' asked the prince.

'I come from where you would like to be,' said the cat.

'And where is that?' said the prince.

'Oh, where is that, indeed! As if I didn't know what you are thinking of, and of whom you are thinking,' said the cat; 'and it would be far better for you to try and save her.'

'I would give my life a thousand times over for her,' said the prince.

'For whom?' said the cat, with a wink. 'I named no name, your highness,' said he.

'You know very well who she is,' said the prince, 'if you knew what I was thinking of; but do you know where she is?'

'She is in danger,' said the cat. 'She is in the castle of the giant Trencoss, in the valley beyond the mountains.'

'I will set out there at once,' said the prince 'and I will challenge the giant to battle and will slay him.'

'Easier said than done,' said the cat. 'There is no sword made by the hands of man can kill him, and even if you could kill him, his hundred hounds, with tongues of fire and claws of iron, would tear you to pieces.'

'Then, what am I to do?' asked the prince.

'Be said by me,' said the cat. 'Go to the wood that surrounds the giant's castle and climb the high tree that's nearest to the window that looks towards the sunset, and shake the branches, and you will see what you will see. Then hold out your hat with the silver plumes, and three balls – one yellow, one red, and one blue – will be thrown into it. And then come back here as fast as you can; but speak no word, for if you utter a single word the hounds will hear you, and you shall be torn to pieces.'

Well, the prince set off at once, and after two days' journey he came to the wood around the castle, and he climbed the tree that was nearest to the window that looked towards the sunset, and he shook the branches.

As soon as he did so, the window opened and he saw the Princess Eileen, looking lovelier than ever. He was going to call out her name, but she placed her fingers on her lips, and he remembered what the cat had told him, that he was to speak no word. In silence, he held out the hat with the silver plumes, and the princess threw into it the three balls, one after another, and, blowing him a kiss, she shut the window.

And well it was she did so, for at that very moment, she heard the voice of the giant, who was coming back from hunting.

The prince waited until the giant had entered the castle before he descended the tree. He set off as fast as he could. He went up hill and down dale, and never stopped until he arrived at his own palace, and there waiting for him was the little white cat.

'Have you brought the three balls?' said he.

'I have,' said the prince.

'Then follow me,' said the cat.

On they went until they left the palace far behind and came to the edge of the sea.

'Now,' said the cat, 'unravel a thread of the red ball, hold the thread in your right hand, drop the ball into the water, and you shall see what you shall see.'

The prince did as he was told, and the ball floated out to sea, unravelling as it went, and it went on until it was out of sight.

'Pull now,' said the cat.

The prince pulled, and, as he did, he saw far away something on the sea shining like silver. It came nearer and nearer, and he saw it was a little silver boat. At last, it touched the strand.

'Now,' said the cat, 'step into this boat and it will bear you to the palace on the island on which no man has ever placed his foot – the island in the unknown seas that were never sailed by vessels made of human hands. In that palace, there is a sword with a diamond hilt, and by that sword alone the giant Trencoss can be killed. There also are a hundred cakes, and it is only on eating these the hundred hounds can die. But mind what I say to you: if you eat or drink until you reach the palace of the little cat in the island in the unknown seas, you will forget the Princess Eileen.'

'I will forget myself first,' said the prince, as he stepped into the silver boat, which floated away so quickly that it was soon out of sight of land.

The day passed and the night fell, and the stars shone down upon the waters, but the boat never stopped. On she went for two whole days and nights, and on the third morning the prince saw an island in the distance, and very glad he was, for he thought it was his journey's end, and he was almost fainting with thirst and hunger. But the day passed, and the island was still before him.

At long last, on the following day, he saw by the first light of the morning that he was quite close to it, and that trees laden with fruit of every kind were bending down over the water. The boat sailed round and round the island, going closer and closer every round, until, at last, the drooping branches almost touched it.

The sight of the fruit within his reach made the prince hungrier and thirstier than he was before and forgetting his promise to the little cat – not to eat anything until he entered the palace in the unknown seas – he caught one of the branches, and, in a moment, was in the tree eating the delicious fruit.

While he was doing so, the boat floated out to sea and soon was lost to sight; but the prince, having eaten, forgot all about it, and, worse still, forgot all about the princess in the giant's castle. When he had eaten enough, he descended the tree, and, turning his back on the sea, set out straight before him.

He had not gone far when he heard the sound of music, and soon after he saw a number of maidens playing on silver harps coming towards him. When they saw him, they ceased playing, and cried out: 'Welcome! Welcome! Prince of the Silver River, welcome to the island of fruits and flowers. Our king and queen saw you coming over the sea, and they sent us to bring you to the palace.'

The prince went with them, and at the palace gates the king and queen and their daughter Kathleen received him and gave him welcome. He hardly saw the king and queen, for his eyes were fixed on the Princess Kathleen, who looked more beautiful than a flower. He thought he had never seen anyone so lovely, for, of course, he had forgotten all about poor Eileen pining away in her castle prison in the lonely valley.

When the king and queen had given welcome to the prince, a great feast was spread, and all the lords and ladies of the court sat down to it, and the prince sat between the queen and the Princess Kathleen, and long before the feast was finished he was overhead and ears in love with her.

When the feast was ended, the queen ordered the ballroom to be made ready, and when night fell, the dancing began, and was kept up until the morning star, and the prince danced all night with the princess, falling deeper and deeper in love with her every minute.

Between dancing by night and feasting by day weeks went by. All the time poor Eileen in the giant's castle was counting the hours, and all this time the dwarfs were winding the balls, and a ball and a half were already wound.

At last, the prince asked the king and queen for their daughter in marriage, and they were delighted to be able to say yes, and the day was fixed for the wedding.

But on the evening before the day on which it was to take place the prince was in his room, getting ready for a dance, when he felt something rubbing against his leg, and, looking down, who should he see but the little white cat.

At the sight of him the prince remembered everything, and sad and sorry he was when he thought of Eileen watching and waiting and counting the days until he returned to save her. But he was very fond of the Princess Kathleen, and so he did not know what to do.

'You can't do anything tonight,' said the cat, for he knew what the prince was thinking of, 'but when morning comes go down to the sea, and look not to the right or the left, and let no living thing touch you, for if you do you shall never leave the island.

Drop the second ball into the water, as you did the first, and when the boat comes, step in at once. Then you may look behind you, and you shall see what you shall see, and you'll know which you love best, the Princess Eileen or the Princess Kathleen, and you can either go or stay.'

The prince didn't sleep a wink that night, and at the first glimpse of the morning he stole from the palace. When he reached the sea, he threw out the ball, and when it had floated out of sight, he saw the little boat sparkling on the horizon like a newly-risen star. The prince had scarcely passed through the palace doors when he was missed, and the king and queen and the princess, and all the lords and ladies of the court, went in search of him, taking the quickest way to the sea.

While the maidens with the silver harps played sweetest music, the princess, whose voice was sweeter than any music, called on the prince by his name, and so moved his heart that he was about to look behind, when he remembered how the cat had told him he should not do so until he was in the boat. Just as it touched the shore, the princess put out her hand and almost caught the prince's arm, but he stepped into the boat in time to save himself, and it sped away like a receding wave.

A loud scream caused the prince to look round suddenly, and when he did, he saw no sign of king or queen, or princess, or lords or ladies, but only big green serpents, with red eyes and tongues, that hissed out fire and poison as they writhed in a hundred horrible coils.

The prince, having escaped from the enchanted island, sailed away for three days and three nights, and every night he hoped the coming morning would show him the island he was in search of. He was faint with hunger and beginning to despair, when on the fourth morning, he saw in the distance an island that, in the first rays of the sun, gleamed like fire.

On coming closer to it, he saw that it was clad with trees, so covered with bright red berries that hardly a leaf was to be seen. Soon, the boat was almost within a stone's cast of the island, and it began to sail round and round until it was well under the bending branches. The scent of the berries was so sweet that it sharpened the prince's hunger, and he longed to pluck them; but, remembering what had happened to him on the enchanted island, he was afraid to touch them.

But the boat kept on sailing round and round, and at last a great wind rose from the sea and shook the branches, and the bright, sweet berries fell into the boat until it was filled with them, and they fell upon the prince's hands, and he took up some to look at them, and as he looked the desire to eat them grew stronger, and he said to himself it would be no harm to taste one; but when he tasted it the flavour was so delicious he swallowed it and, of course, at once he forgot all about Eileen, and the boat drifted away from him and left him standing in the water.

He climbed on to the island, and having eaten enough of the berries, he set out to see what might be before him, and it was not long until he heard a great noise, and a huge iron ball knocked down one of the trees in front of him, and before he knew where he was a hundred giants came running after it.

When they saw the prince, they turned towards him, and one of them caught him up in his hand and held him up that all might see him. The prince was nearly squeezed to death and seeing this the giant put him on the ground again.

'Who are you, my little man?' asked the giant.

'I am a prince,' replied the prince.

'Oh, you are a prince, are you?' said the giant. 'And what are you good for?' said he.

The prince did not know, for nobody had asked him that question before.

'I know what he's good for,' said an old giantess, with one eye in her forehead and one in her chin. 'I know what he's good for. He's good to eat.'

When the giants heard this, they laughed so loud that the prince was frightened almost to death.

'Why,' said one, 'he wouldn't make a mouthful.'

'Oh, leave him to me,' said the giantess, 'and I'll fatten him up; and when he is cooked and dressed, he will be a nice dainty dish for the king.'

The giants, on this, gave the prince into the hands of the old giantess. She took him home with her to the kitchen and fed him on sugar and spice and all things nice, so that he should be a sweet morsel for the king of the giants when he returned to the island. The poor prince would not eat anything at first, but the giantess held him over the fire until his feet were scorched, and then he said to himself it was better to eat than to be burnt alive.

Well, day after day passed, and the prince grew sadder and sadder, thinking that he would soon be cooked and dressed for the king; but sad as the prince was, he was not half as sad as the Princess Eileen in the giant's castle, watching and waiting for the prince to return and save her.

And the dwarfs had wound two balls and were winding a third.

At last, the prince heard from the old giantess that the king of the giants was to return on the following day, and she said to him: 'As this is the last night you have to live, tell me if you wish for anything, for if you do, your wish will be granted.'

'I don't wish for anything,' said the prince, whose heart was dead within him.

'Well, I'll come back again,' said the giantess, and she went away.

The prince sat down in a corner, thinking and thinking, until he heard close to his ear a sound like 'purr, purr!' He looked around, and there before him was the little white cat.

'I ought not to come to you,' said the cat; 'but, indeed, it is not for your sake I come. I come for the sake of the Princess Eileen. Of course, you forgot all about her, and, of course, she is always thinking of you. It's always the way,

"Favoured lovers may forget, Slighted lovers never yet."'

The prince blushed with shame when he heard the name of the princess.

"Tis you that ought to blush,' said the cat; 'but listen to me now, and remember, if you don't obey my directions this time, you'll never see me again, and you'll never set your eyes on the Princess Eileen. When the old giantess comes back, tell her you wish, when the morning comes, to go down to the sea to look at it for the last time. When you reach the sea, you will know what to do. But I must go now, as I hear the giantess coming.'

And the cat jumped out of the window and disappeared.

'Well,' said the giantess, when she came in, 'is there anything you wish?'

'Is it true I must die tomorrow?' asked the prince.

'It is.'

'Then,' said he, 'I should like to go down to the sea to look at it for the last time.'

'You may do that,' said the giantess, 'if you get up early.'

'I'll be up with the lark in the light of the morning,' said the prince.

'Very well,' said the giantess, and, saying 'good night,' she went away.

The prince thought the night would never pass, but at last, it faded away before the grey light of the dawn, and he sped down to the sea. He threw out the third ball, and before long, he saw the little boat coming towards him swifter than the wind. He threw himself into it the moment it touched the shore.

Swifter than the wind it bore him out to sea, and before he had time to look behind him the island of the giantess was like a faint red speck in the distance. The day passed and the night fell, and the stars looked down, and the boat sailed on, and just as the sun rose above the sea it pushed its silver prow on the golden strand of an island greener than the leaves in summer. The prince jumped out and went on and on until he entered a pleasant valley, at the head of which he saw a palace white as snow.

As he approached the central door, it opened for him. On entering the hall, he passed into several rooms without meeting with anyone; but, when he reached the principal apartment, he found himself in a circular room, in which were a thousand pillars, and every pillar was of marble, and on every pillar save one, which stood in the centre of the room, was a little white cat with black eyes.

Ranged round the wall, from one doorjamb to the other, were three rows of precious jewels. The first was a row of brooches of gold and silver, with their pins fixed in the wall and their heads outwards; the second a row of torques of gold and silver; and the third a row of great swords, with hilts of gold and silver. And on many tables was food of all kinds, and drinking horns filled with foaming ale.

While the prince was looking about him, the cats kept on jumping from pillar to pillar; but seeing that none of them jumped on to the pillar in the centre of the room, he began to wonder why this was so, when, all of a sudden, and before he could guess how it came about, there right before him on the centre pillar was the little white cat.

'Don't you know me?' said he.

'I do,' said the prince.

'Ah, but you don't know who I am. This is the palace of the Little White Cat, and I am the king of the Cats. But you must be hungry, and the feast is spread.'

Well, when the feast was ended, the king of the cats called for the sword that would kill the giant Trencoss, and the hundred cakes for the hundred watchdogs.

The cats brought the sword and the cakes and laid them before the king.

'Now,' said the king, 'take these; you have no time to lose. Tomorrow, the dwarfs will wind the last ball, and tomorrow the giant will claim the princess for his bride. So, you should go at once; but before you go, take this from me to your little girl.'

And the king gave him a brooch lovelier than any on the palace walls.

The king and the prince, followed by the cats, went down to the strand, and when the prince stepped into the boat, all the cats 'mewed' three times for good luck, and the prince waved his hat three times, and the little boat sped over the waters all through the night as brightly and as swiftly as a shooting star.

In the first flush of the morning, it touched the strand. The prince jumped out and went on and on, uphill and down dale, until he came to the giant's castle. When the hounds saw him, they barked furiously, and bounded towards him to tear him to pieces.

The prince flung the cakes to them, and as each hound swallowed his cake, he fell dead. The prince then struck his shield three times with the sword which he had brought from the palace of the little white cat.

When the giant heard the sound, he cried out: 'Who comes to challenge me on my wedding day?'

The dwarfs went out to see, and, returning, told him it was a prince who challenged him to battle.

The giant, foaming with rage, seized his heaviest iron club, and rushed out to the fight. The fight lasted the whole day, and when the sun went down the giant said: 'We have had enough of fighting for the day. We can begin at sunrise tomorrow.'

'Not so,' said the prince. 'Now or never; win or die.'

'Then take this,' cried the giant, as he aimed a blow with all his force at the prince's head; but the prince, darting forward like a flash of lightning, drove his sword into the giant's heart, and, with a groan, he fell over the bodies of the poisoned hounds.

When the dwarfs saw the giant dead, they began to cry and tear their hair. But the prince told them they had nothing to fear, and he bade them go and tell the Princess Eileen he wished to speak with her.

But the princess had watched the battle from her window, and when she saw the giant fall, she rushed out to greet the prince, and that very night he and she and all the dwarfs and harpers set out for the palace of the Silver River, which they reached the next morning, and from that day to this, there never has been a more glorious wedding than the wedding of the prince of the Silver River and the Princess Eileen; and though she had diamonds and pearls to spare, the only jewel she wore on her wedding-day was the brooch which the prince had brought her from the palace of the Little White Cat in the far-off seas.

From: Irish Fairy Tales

Finis

Workbooks From The Scheherazade Foundation

We hope that you have enjoyed this collection of stories, gleaned from varying cultural corners of the world, and that you have been entertained by them.

But, have you considered the deeper meanings and interwoven layers that lie hidden beneath the surface?

At The Scheherazade Foundation, we believe that Teaching-Stories contain wisdom, information, and marvels that have the power to transform the way we think, and thereby change our lives.

Employed as a bedrock of culture throughout the centuries – challenging established patterns of thinking, while passing on knowledge and values – tales such as the ones contained in this volume are a rich resource ready and waiting to be mined.

As an aid to help in the perception of less-obvious facets and layers, we have created a series of original Workbooks. Aimed at stimulating thought-provoking discussions and igniting deep reflection, these tools will assist in unlocking the power of Teaching-Stories.